KARA'S WOLVES

WOLF MASTERS, BOOK ONE

BECCA JAMESON

ACKNOWLEDGMENTS

To my readers who made this book soar and begged me to turn this into a series. I never could have imagined the success you all have brought me with a few wolves and some inspiration!

CHAPTER 1

"This is *so* not a good idea." Kara Shepherd leaned back against Lindsey's dusty red Toyota and stared down at the gravel parking lot. A cool evening Oregon breeze, typical for May, blew the dust around between the cars. "Why did I let you two talk me into this?" Kara scraped the toe of her new Durango boots through the rocks and nearly laughed out loud as her gaze roamed up her body to take in the entire package. Her roommates, Lindsey and Jessica, both bombshells, hauled her scrawny ass into Cavender's that afternoon for the new country-western wear she was outfitted in—low-rise boot-cut jeans, a short white blouse tied in a knot just below her breasts, and the stiff awkward boots that would take weeks of wear to break in. Her feet, unaccustomed to shoes of any kind, were already begging to be let loose from their confines.

"Come on." Lindsey pinned her gaze on Kara. "It's already almost nine o'clock."

Lindsey looked at home in her own newly purchased duds. Every curve molded to get the best effect from her tight blue jeans and skimpy tank top. There was nothing wrong with Kara's look, but at five feet she was six to seven inches shorter than her friends and looked much younger than her age.

From out of nowhere, Lindsey and Jessica flanked Kara on both sides. Each grabbed an arm and practically dragged her toward the entrance to the country bar. Kara released a squeal in protest that blended with the twangy music leaking through the walls of the joint all the way out into the parking lot.

"I don't know how to two-step or line dance, don't drink or smoke and have listened to country music less than a handful of times in my life. Why are we here?" she whined. A knot in the pit of her stomach twisted at the thought of entering the crowded, smoke-filled, loud, God-awful dance hall.

Jess's cheerful laughter filled the night air. "That's the whole point, Kara. You need to get out more. Four years we've been going to Oregon State, and you've spent the entire time like a robot, going from class to the gym to the apartment, and back to class, and then to the gym and back to the apartment—"

"I get the idea," Kara mumbled.

"We're about to graduate." Jess showed a mouth full of perfect, white teeth. In fact, everything about the tall, slender woman was perfect. "It's time to live a little. Maybe even...*gasp*...meet a man."

"Oh, no." Kara planted her feet into the loose gravel, struggling to break her friends' hold. "Is that what this is all about?" Their grips on her arms tightened. "Don't tell me you have someone all lined up in there. I'll kill you both. I'm just fine, thank you very much. And far too busy for dating." Her friends were not going to let her get away.

"No, Kara..." Lindsey began, "...we didn't arrange a blind date or anything, although I do wish we had thought of it. Next time..." Lindsey glanced over at Kara and laughed. "You should see your horrified expression."

Her cheeks were burning hot and beads of perspiration were threatening to burst out above her brows.

"Look, we're just going to go inside," Jess quickly chimed in, "get a table and have a good time. Okay?" She pulled again on Kara's arm. Kara looked down at her friend's grasp. If she didn't relinquish control soon, she would end up with bruises on both sides of her body. How would she explain that to her coach Monday morning?

Oh, yeah, those bruises? Well, Coach, my girlfriends were dragging me out to a bar and...

"*Fine*. But I don't want to stay long. I have to study tomorrow, early." Kara took a deep breath, shook herself free of her captors, and let her shoulders fall into a more relaxed stance. She inhaled another breath of courage. "Let's get this over with," she mumbled as she made her way to the entrance, reaching into her pocket for her ID. At twenty-one, Kara's small stature and youthful looks always made her age extremely questionable. Not that she had many occasions in the past to demonstrate her drinking age.

Lindsey pasted on a huge smile. "Now that's what I'm talking about." She pulled the door open and, flourishing a low bow, allowed her friends to proceed inside.

The bar was wall-to-wall people, an ocean of Stetsons of every color. Even the dance floor was jammed. Loud sad tones of some slow country song filled the air, vibrating the floor beneath Kara's feet. Kara had no idea this place even existed just outside Corvallis. She followed behind Jess toward a tall round bar table meant purely as a place to set your drink while dancing. The tables were spaced all around the dance floor, but none of them had stools to sit on. Hell, there wasn't even room to sit in this establishment. It was going to be a long night.

∿

Justin Masters paused, his beer midway to his lips. "Fuck. Fuck, fuck, and damn. I don't believe this." He slammed the nearly full beer down on the table, foam frothing up and running over the sides of the bottle like a waterfall to cover the hand white-knuckling the glass.

Ryan, his closest brother in age, startled at the line of expletives. "What? Dude? What's gotten into you?"

Justin raised his head, closed his eyes and took a long, slow, inhale of air into his lungs. "Mother fucker." His skin crawled, his cock jumped to attention, and his clothes suddenly felt way too tight for his body. He struggled to control the impulse to change.

When Justin finally opened his eyes, he found himself staring straight into Ryan's grinning face. "She's here, isn't she?"

Of course his brother would know exactly what was going on. They knew each other like the back of their own hands. The only other person in the world who would have also been on the same page as Justin was Trevor. And Trevor would not be happy when he found out about tonight.

At twenty-eight years old, Trevor Shields and Justin had been sharing women for nearly half their lives. In a race against time, each had been hoping to make it into their thirties before finding their mates. This new development shot that idea to hell.

Justin shook his head at Ryan. "I'm not ready. I wanted more time. I—"

"Dude. It doesn't work that way and you know it." Ryan

laughed outright now. His wavy brown hair, identical to Justin's, fell across his eyes, covering some of the mirth. He scanned the jam-packed room. "Where is she? Do you see her yet? Is she hot?"

Justin lowered his gaze to the table. "I don't know." His sticky, beer-covered hand shook. He let go of the bottle to flick his fingers by his side and shake off the foam. "I'm afraid to look."

The chuckling beside him continued. "Bro, you can't stop fate. You're going to have to face the music... Come on. Let's go find her." Ryan picked up his beer and motioned with his head for Justin to follow him.

Taking another deep breath to steady himself, Justin grudgingly grabbed his bottle and downed the entire contents while Ryan waited with a wide smirk Justin had half a mind to physically erase.

"Feel better?" Ryan was obviously loving this.

"No, smartass. I do not feel better." *Why now? Why tonight?*

Exasperated, Justin stared at Ryan, who raised his eyebrows under his dark locks of hair as if to say, "Well? What are you waiting for?"

"Okay, okay." Justin led the way through the crowded throng of line dancers in the direction of the powerful scent of his mate which stood out above all other smells of perfume, sweat, deodorant and aftershave permeating the confined area of the bar. His wolf hovered just beneath the surface, demanding to find his mate. It was a process as old as time. There was no avoiding it. "Not now" was not an answer.

Meandering through the crowd was slow work. Surely the place was above the legal occupancy quota tonight, or was it that his skin was crawling each time he brushed by another person? Justin had never seen so many people at

Boot Scooters before, and he came here a lot. He and Trevor usually had no problem finding a woman willing to engage in the kind of sex play they enjoyed.

As if choreographed, the crowd parted, and there she stood. Justin came to a dead stop, causing Ryan to slam into the back of him.

"I'm guessing you found her?" Laughter still filled Ryan's voice.

Dammit. This is not a joke.

Whatever trepidation Justin felt moments ago evaporated into thin air. Standing with her back to him, just a few yards away, was the sexiest woman he had ever laid eyes on, assuming of course, her ass was no false advertisement for her face. Then again, you could tell a lot about a woman by just looking at her ass, and this one was a beauty. Justin sucked in a breath and held it as he beheld the tiny sprite who had no idea her world was about to change completely and irrevocably.

Barely five feet tall, she had long blonde curls reaching way down her back. Justin ached to tangle his hands in those glorious locks. Jeans hung low on her slender hips to hug her sexy firm ass to perfection. Her slight waist was bare between her short blouse and formfitting jeans. Justin shivered at the thought of wrapping his huge hands around her warm middle. He could probably touch the tips of his fingers on each side. He and Trevor would completely swallow her up.

Shit, Trevor. The thought of sharing this sexy mate of his did not sit well with Justin. *Where is this possessiveness coming from?* Plus, she did not look like the kind of girl who liked to be shared. Her stance was shy between her girlfriends, but her backbone was tense, screaming she did not want to be here. Nothing like the usual women Justin liked to spend the evening with—women who held their heads high, thrust their breasts out, and all but begged to be taken. Hell, he'd never seen his mate out anywhere before, and he knew for a fact she had never been any place he frequented. He would have caught her scent hanging in the air.

This close, Justin could almost taste her sweet essence on the tip of his tongue. He stood there rigid. He would never forget this moment.

Ryan whispered close to Justin's ear, "Are you just going to stand there and stare at her all night? Ask her to dance."

"I'm...observing her. Patience, man. She's a human. She's...not expecting this," Justin muttered under his breath, his lips barely moving, as if she would somehow hear him over the constant bass beat surrounding them.

"Others have mated with humans. They got over it. This woman will, too." Were those words supposed to make Justin feel better? He was about to rock the world off its axis for this sexy vixen. He took a long slow breath deep into his lungs. She smelled so...innocent. It had certainly been a while since she'd been with a man. There was no trace of another mixed with her scent. She deserved a little...respect. *Right, keep telling yourself that, asshole. She doesn't even know about your sorry ass yet. You're just plain chickenshit.*

Justin made a quick about face and headed to the bar, Ryan hot on his heels. "What are you doing, man?"

"What does it look like I'm doing? Getting a drink, okay? Do I need your permission to get a drink?" *Cut me some slack.*

Ryan resumed chuckling. "You're *scared... Ha...* You *are.*" This was way too funny for Ryan and it was beginning to wear on Justin's nerves.

"Look, let me handle this. My way. Back off. Go...go find someone to dance with or something." Justin glared over his shoulder at Ryan. Apparently his look was sufficiently harsh, because Ryan held up both hands in surrender and slowly backed away toward the dance floor. His low laugh did not, however, disappear for several seconds.

"Give me a shot of Jack and a Budweiser," Justin nearly shouted at the bartender. *I can't hear myself think in this room.* He tugged at the collar of his western shirt. Was it not stiflingly hot in here?

He didn't have to turn around to know the gorgeous little fairy behind him had not moved an inch. His nose would keep him updated on her whereabouts. When the bartender returned, Justin slapped a ten on the bar, chugged the whisky, and turned to lean his back against the rail, tipping his beer back with one hand to chase the burning liquor down his throat.

Hopefully the drink would help control both his raging hard on as well as his shaking anxiety. It didn't work. When he brought his vision back to center, he paused dead in his tracks. When had she gotten closer? There she was, staring straight at him.

"Excuse me? Could you um…" She was pointing at the bar behind him.

Justin was still as a statue, holding his breath. *What a fox. My God. Thank you, Lord.* Her face turned up toward him and she sucked in a breath. Her brows shot upward and then settled back into place. Her dainty finger pointed to his right, but he couldn't take his gaze off her angelic face. Her full mouth curved at a questioning angle. Wide, bright blue eyes like the ocean. Staring into them would surely make him seasick. Her blonde curls fell over her shoulders in a cascade of silk. He had to hold himself in check to keep from reaching out to take a lock in his hand and bury his face in it.

Shit. Move, man. Say something. You look like a fool. Justin exhaled. "Sorry. Sorry."

Maybe she wants to order a drink? Right, of course. *This is a bar after all. People walk up to the counter and they order beverages. You're blocking the front line.* "Can I…um…get you something?" He looked at her expression of apprehension and decided to take a different angle. "I mean…it's hard to get the bartender's attention in all this confusion. I'd be happy to wave him down and order for you… If you'd like?" *Please say yes.*

Justin automatically reached for her slender arm, pulling her away from the line of drunk bastards about to stumble into her. Too late. They managed to slam her forward anyway and she squished gloriously flat against him, awakening every nerve ending in his body. Sparks lit up his system.

"Oh." She gasped in shock and jumped back a step as though he had just poked her with a hot iron.

Justin still had a hold of her amazingly firm biceps, unwilling to release her. "Are you okay? I was trying to pull you out of the way in time, but I guess I failed." He tried to flash her a playful smile, but doubted the intent would be obvious.

"I'm fine. No… I mean yes… I'm fine… Thanks." She looked down at the floor a moment before once again raising her sky blue gaze back to his. She had to tip her head way back to stare up at his face. He was more than a foot taller than her.

Everything lines up in bed… With Trevor at her back and… *Shit.* He needed to lose that line of thinking fast. Matings between three people were almost unheard of, and a threesome was surely the furthest thing from her mind.

She was aroused though, and shocked by it, if the look

on her face was anything to go by. He could smell it on her. She surely knew nothing about bonding with wolves or matings. But, he realized, she would not be able to avoid the pull of her body to his. In a matter of days, she would be unable to deny him. Her body would crave the bonding, even without understanding. It was fated. They would be together.

"What can I get you?" Justin leaned in closer to her and breathed in the most glorious fragrance of floral shampoo and her personal essence—honeysuckle with a faint edge of...chalk? *Is she a teacher?* Did they even use chalkboards anymore?

"Huh?" She seemed momentarily disoriented. That was a good sign. Hopefully she was focused so much on her attraction to him, she couldn't remember what she'd come over here for in the first place. "Oh, right. A drink. Can you order me a mineral water please?" She smiled.

A mineral water? "Um, sure..." Justin relaxed the grip he still had on her arm just a fraction, with no intention of letting go altogether. Keeping one eye trained on her, he angled his head toward the bar and waited a beat to get the man's attention.

"Can you get me a...mineral water?"

Without a glance in his direction, the waiter placed a green bottle in front of Justin. "It's on the house."

Justin reached behind himself with his free hand and grasped the cold drink, sweat dripping off the label to coat his heated palm.

Sparks once again tingled up Justin's arm when their fingers met to pass off the beverage. He didn't want to stop touching her. In fact, he wanted to pull her closer again. Flatten her against his chest. Tuck her head against him and run his hands through her golden hair...

"Thanks." She pulled away from him. Before he could

form a sentence, she had retreated toward her friends, her back to him, her fantastic ass swaying enticingly.

Justin smiled from his perch at the bar. Thank God the sturdy edge was there to hold him up. The sweet scent of her arousal stirred his senses. He grinned. She was just as turned on as he. His skin heated. He would need to run miles in the woods tonight to work off the sexual tension building in his body. There was no way in hell he was going to be able to take her tonight. No. It would take some gentle courting to steer her in the right direction. His earlier stress had faded however. His fate was sealed. She was his.

CHAPTER 2

Kara sauntered back to her friends with a grin on her face, her head held a little higher than before. Whoever the guy was, he was hot. And, he found *her* attractive. The thought made her pulse race and gave her a little more pep in her step, perhaps a slight sway to her hips as she walked.

There was no way to tell if the cowboy get-up was just for tonight, or if he woke up every day to pull his boots on under his Levi's. Whatever the case may be, the result was one hunk of sexy manhood. Heat crept up her cheeks with the memory of his firm erection pressed into her stomach when she fell into him. *Did I do that?*

Lindsey eyed her suspiciously. "What happened to you? It took forever and—" She paused. "Why are you smiling?" Her perfectly arched eyebrows rose.

What? Did her friends not think her capable of luring a man? Kara was feeling far too smug to be slighted by either of their shocked expressions.

"Did you just flirt with that guy at the bar?" Jessica's jaw dropped at the question. She glanced back and forth between Kara and the bar behind her.

"What guy?" Surely they hadn't seen her or paid attention.

"The one still staring at your ass with drool running down his chin," Lindsey continued.

Kara jerked her head around to confirm he was indeed ogling her like a piece of candy. She gave a flirtatious smile in his direction and turned back to face her roommates. "I guess I did."

Heat radiated from her toes to her cheeks, probably making embarrassing splotchy patterns on her face and neck. Her pale skin always had that reaction at the first sign of stress.

"Well, see? I rest my case. I told you. You need to get out more often. The men in here are itching to get a chance. And we just got here." Jess gave a cute little fake pout.

Kara would have sworn she heard the faint sound of jealousy in her friend's voice.

Jess was the most outgoing of the three women. She lived life much closer to the edge than Kara ever dreamed. Her stylish hair was cropped short and spiked with blonde highlights tipping the ends. Several earrings dangled from the piercings in both ears. Her flirtatious laugh always managed to draw men close to her. Not that it did them any good because Jess blew them all off. She hadn't dated anyone for as long as Kara had known her.

Lindsey, on the other hand, was more like Kara. Her long straight brown hair reached midway down her back and her big brown eyes could lure anyone in, but she was softer spoken than Jess, a perfect balance.

"I dare you to go dance with him." Jess bubbled over with excitement.

"No way. We just got here. I don't even know how to two-step." Kara shook her head, unable to stop the motion. Her ears heated at the forward thought.

"Double dare you." Now Lindsey was ganging up on her, too.

"How about..." Jess paused, her fingers tapping her chin, to ponder the ceiling. "I've got it. How about a bet? If you can get him to dance with you, which is a shoo-in by the way, we'll do all the household chores for a week."

Oh, she looks so proud of herself.

"Seriously? You two would clean the bathroom and the kitchen for an entire week just to get me to ask a guy to dance?" It sounded crazy, but then again, these two knew the likelihood of Kara being so bold was slim to none. On the flipside, this was the last week of school. A few less duties would free her up to study for finals.

They both nodded in unison and folded their arms across their chests.

What harm could it do? What was the worst that could happen?

Kara slowly turned her gaze in the direction of the man still perched against the bar to find him staring straight at her with a smile on his face. His stance looked stiff. He was trying too hard. She smiled to herself and couldn't help the slow perusal of his body her eyes insisted upon. His face was shaded from this angle with his suede cowboy hat leaning over his forehead. He had surely just picked up his pressed charcoal shirt from the drycleaners. As her gaze moved south, she found his jeans hugged him to perfection. And what perfection. A shiver ran through her as she remembered having been plastered to him only moments before. Kara tried to shake the image by continuing her meandering gaze to his boots. Worn. Not brand-new, purchased-today, stiff and shiny, like her own.

Could she go through with this? *Shit. Why not?* An entire week of rest and relaxation from apartment duties for just one dance with a hot hunk? Who wouldn't?

"Fine." Without turning back to face her friends, Kara set her bottle on the edge of the table and traipsed back in the direction of the hottest guy in the bar. Did he have to be such a stud? It would have been so much easier if he had been just a regular patron.

~

Damn. The little pixie was heading back his way with a slightly hesitant look on her face, her sexy, full bottom lip between her teeth. Justin's dick jumped to attention. He wanted to pull that soft lip into his mouth and worry it a little with his own teeth.

When she stood before him, she began to stammer. "Um… I can't… I mean, I can't dance…"

Why is she telling me this?

"What I mean is… You see…" She chewed on her bottom lip.

He loved the flustered look on her face and had no intention whatsoever of putting her out of her misery, even if he could decipher what she was trying desperately to communicate.

A sudden spark of electricity raised the hairs on his arms. His skin crawled with the need to touch her again; to verify the sparks had not been his imagination. *Patience, Justin. You're going to need a bucket full of patience for the next several days.*

She was going to gnaw a hole in her lip if she kept that up.

Justin smiled at her and waited.

"My friends," she turned to point in the direction she had clearly come from, "bet me I couldn't get you to dance with me."

Justin chuckled. *Really? How convenient.* They had no

idea what was about to happen to their sweet, innocent friend and they had bet her to dance with him? Nice.

"I mean… You don't have to…of course." She rolled her eyes toward the ceiling, clearly flustered. "Are you waiting on someone?" She glanced around the bar as it dawned on her that perhaps he wasn't alone.

Time to put her out of her misery. "I would be honored, ma'am." Justin gave a short bow and reached out to grasp the dainty fingers of the woman he was going to spend the rest of his life loving. The sparks kept flying.

Without further preamble, Justin whispered a prayer of gratitude to whatever gods were hanging around the dance floor tonight and gently pulled his sweet little mate toward the circle of two-steppers.

"I um…don't actually…know how to dance," she mumbled behind him as they reached the edge of the wood floor.

"You mentioned that." Pulling her in front of him, he tucked one finger under her chin and tilted her face up to stare directly into her glorious eyes. "Don't worry. *I* do."

She swallowed. Justin's heart squeezed.

"Just follow my lead." His double entendre was only for himself.

At the edge of the dance floor, Justin placed the cool palm of her left hand on his shoulder and grasped her right hand in his left. His giant fingers completely swallowed her tiny ones. He stared for a moment at her smooth fair skin contrasting against his rough, sun-darkened tones. Short clipped fingernails, filed to perfection, graced her dainty hand, but her palm was callused. *Does she work in construction?* He almost laughed out loud at the thought and then decided she must surely enjoy gardening or something.

When Justin wrapped his right arm around Kara's

shoulder, he noticed she was not a fragile rose by any stretch of the imagination. She may have been small, but she was incredibly muscular. How did this wisp of a woman manage to maintain such strength?

"Um, what do I do now?" Kara was staring up at him again, her eyes questioning. How long had they been standing there? He wasn't sure.

"Right. Well, the basic steps are very simple. It's a series of slow, slow, quick, quick." Justin edged them into the line of traffic. "Our feet will move together. When I step back, you step forward on the same side. Feel the music. The beat is always a steady slow, slow, quick, quick."

Kara caught on fast. She didn't seem to falter at his instructions. Thank God, because he could barely think with her in his arms, her face so close to his chest, her scent permeating the air around him.

"You're a natural. Didn't you say you'd never two-stepped before?"

"Yes… I mean no, I haven't. I'll probably step on you in a minute." Her smile sucked the air out of Justin. Time to bump this relationship up a notch.

"I'm Justin, by the way. Justin Masters."

"Kara Shepherd. Do you, um, go to school here?"

"No. I mean, I did." *Don't tell her your age yet, you doofus.* "But, I graduated. I work on a dairy farm now, just outside of town. You?"

"I graduate this May. Teaching degree."

Sexy and educated. *Why haven't I ever seen her before?*

The music switched to a slow song and Justin let his right hand trail down Kara's back to rest on her bare waist and draw her closer. He could reach so far around her his fingers grazed her firm abs. Her skin felt cool beneath his touch and she gave a short gasp at the contact with his warm hands.

17

"Kara…" He loved that name. Delicate, but strong. It suited her perfectly.

"Yes?"

Had he spoken out loud?

Justin chuckled to himself just as someone graciously bumped into Kara from behind, forcing her body flush against his. For the second time tonight. He held her tighter, causing the vibrations of laughter to run through his chest and into hers.

He had always prided himself on being firm and fit—most of his kind were—but this tiny lady could rival him in the fitness department. She was rock solid. Her small breasts brushed against his chest as he laughed at himself.

"Sorry, I was just trying out your name. Didn't realize I had spoken out loud."

Justin cautiously set Kara's right hand on his shoulder, freeing himself to reach around her with both hands at her waist, trapping her in a slow sensuous dance. Their movements were barely existent among the crowd. Justin didn't care. If he died right now, it would be worth it.

"Well, Justin Masters," she peered up at him, a soft curl falling across her face, "you're a fantastic dancer. Thanks for showing me the ropes."

Honey, you haven't begun to experience my ropes.

Justin cleared his throat, trying to shake the image of Kara with her delicate wrists tied to his bedposts while he held her legs apart and sucked on her clit. The vision included his buddy Trevor pinching her nipples into tight buds above him. Would she be a screamer?

"No problem." Justin found himself physically shaking the image from his head. His mate was completely unaware she was about to be claimed. By at least one man. The images of him and Trevor sharing her would not shake. Was it possible she would belong to them both?

One song ended and another sultry ballad began. Shania Twain's voice filled the room now, her words caressing them as they swayed to the beat. Justin's chest swelled when she didn't seem to notice they were now moving on to a third song. If she hadn't been interested, she would have quickly pulled away after the first. Of course, there was no way she could "not be interested." It was fated after all.

"So, Kara. What do you do when you're not in class? I don't think I've ever seen you here before."

"Actually, I'm a gymnast. Well, until next week anyway. My career is about to come to an end."

Ah, that explains the physique. Wait…a gymnast? As in flipping around on the ground, flying through the air, attempting suicidal feats not meant for womankind to endure? Justin sucked in a breath, his fingers gripping her waist. Why did visions of her tumbling cause him distress?

"Really?" He couldn't eke out any other syllables at the moment. Tendrils of horrible images flitted through his mind.

"I've been working in the gym several hours a day for almost my entire life. Next weekend I'll have my last gymnastics meet and become a free woman. That's why I'm here tonight actually. My roommates think they need to indoctrinate me into society, so to speak." A sexy giggle bubbled from her chest. "They say I never have any fun. So, they dragged me out here and then bribed me to get on the dance floor. And here we are."

She made it sound so simple. Just a few more days of school and gymnastics, and she would be all his. He shivered at the thought. Trevor was definitely not going to like this new twist. Justin may be a doting protective man to have around, but Trevor was off the charts when it came to safety. Maybe he could manage to keep the two of them from meeting for a few weeks, buy some time?

Not a chance in hell.

Justin's mind was so connected to Trevor's, he was probably on his way here now, just buzzing with the mental vibrations rushing through their link. He tried to block their connection as best he could.

"Do you have *any* free time? I'd sure like to take you out on a proper date." *What if she says no?* Justin didn't want to have to force the issue, but the reality was she was his now and he was not going to take kindly to letting her out of his sight very often.

"Well…" she appeared to be pondering the idea, nibbling once again on that lower lip of hers "…I guess I do eat, occasionally. Perhaps dinner sometime?"

Thank God she wasn't just going to blow him off. "How's tomorrow? Six o'clock? I'll pick you up?" Justin held his breath waiting on her response.

"Tomorrow? Hmm…" She glanced up at him and he read unease in her eyes. "I hardly know you at all. Maybe I could meet you somewhere?"

"Sure." It had been a while since Justin had spent any real time with a human woman. He'd forgotten they could be a little nervous about dating. Secretly, he was glad to find she would be a little cautious. He and Trevor did frequently sleep with non-shifters, but not the timid type standing before him right now, gnawing on a lip he badly wanted to soothe with his own tongue. "How about we meet at the Steak House on First Street. Do you know it?" A steak could go a long way toward soothing his need to sink his teeth into Kara's supple young skin, perhaps chew on a nipple or nip her tight little clit between his teeth.

"Steak?" There was a hint of surprise in her voice. "Um, okay."

What? Don't tell me she's a vegetarian. That would be disastrous.

"I can find it. First Street you said?" Her tongue darted out to lick the edges of her mouth nervously.

Justin craved to kiss the worry from her. "Yes, just a block down from the mall."

He held his breath, knowing she was in control of this situation, but he had to make some concessions to ease her mind. She was a human. New territory for him. He wasn't used to tiptoeing around a woman. At least now that he'd found her, he knew she could never escape him. With his sense of smell he could track her wherever she might go. Her essence now permeated his soul.

Someone bumped them from behind and Justin realized they had stopped moving. With a short sidestep, he moved them off the dance floor.

Kara looked up at him with questioning eyes.

He couldn't stand being this close to her another moment without tasting her. He cupped the side of Kara's face. "God, I want to kiss you."

Justin half-expected her to turn and walk away. Instead, she gazed into his eyes and whispered, "Yes," so softly he almost didn't hear her.

"Not here. Outside. Do you trust me?" He didn't want their first glorious kiss to be in this crowded room.

"Uhm, hm. I don't know why..." She looked at him with such faith, a shiver coursed through him. He had no idea what the effect of finding a mate would be on a human. Was she as entranced as he?

"Come on..." Justin grabbed her by the hand and led her across the room. He was going to combust if he didn't at least get a taste of her before he allowed her to leave this evening.

She didn't yank her hand away. He could smell the

slight tinge of fear, but she was also aroused by him, her body already taking control of her reactions. Once they actually mated, she would never be able to deny him again. Her pussy would beg and plead for his cock. But for now, she was just getting a taste of the need that would soon drive her bonkers.

~

Kara wanted to pull from the grasp Justin had on her hand, really she did. Her mind was shouting "No," but her traitorous body was screaming "Yes."

She was mesmerized by the way he looked into her eyes, seemed to peer into her soul, the way he had held her possessively in his arms and stroked her bare skin beneath her blouse, the way his low rumbling voice reached into her heart... She was unable to stop herself from following him to whatever destination he had in mind. It was mad. That was a fact. No woman in their right mind would allow a strange man to lead them away from the safety of their friends and...out into the night? *Shit.*

He led her right out the front door and before she could utter a syllable, she found herself against the side of the building, his strong, huge body melding against her and his lips lowering toward hers. Kara gasped and gripped his biceps with both hands as he took her mouth in a fiery kiss that sent a shiver clear down to her feet.

No one had ever kissed her like this. Granted, she could count on one hand the number of men she had even kissed at all, but none of them had elicited this...this...burn grasping her sex.

Justin tipped his head slightly to one side and deepened the kiss, tracing her lips with his tongue before dipping it into her mouth to tangle and dance with her own. He tasted of beer and mint and kissed her with an urgency she was beginning to feel herself.

Strong hands circled her waist, his thumbs rubbing a pattern of circles on her stomach, driving her crazy with new sensations of need.

Slowly Justin's palms moved upward until they grazed the bottom of Kara's breasts beneath the lace bra she wore. She should be pushing him away. Why was she letting a stranger fondle her like this? All she knew was she wanted more. More of his touch. More of his kisses. Liquid pooled between her legs to dampen her panties. A tingling sensation shot from the spot where his fingers barely brushed against her breasts straight down to her sex.

A low moan escaped her and she gasped, jerking her head back into the wall when she realized it was her.

Justin placed his forehead against hers and chuckled lightly, a tone she was beginning to find increasingly arousing.

"Are you okay?" He ran a hand through her hair.

He probably meant to soothe her, but she couldn't for the life of her remember why. She just knew she never wanted him to stop touching her. Her hips pushed forward of their own accord, straight into his rock-hard thigh. With one leg strategically placed between hers, his erection was burning a hot line of need against her.

Kara jumped when a door slammed into the wall to her right, allowing loud raucous noise to escape the confines of the bar and spread out into the cool night air, forcing Kara's mind back to earth. How long had they been standing here? Surely only moments.

She peered around Justin's massive biceps to catch Lindsey and Jess falling out the door, staggering to catch their breath as their gazes jerked from one end of the parking lot to the other. Just as Kara suspected. Her protective friends would never allow her to leave with a stranger. It warmed her heart to know they cared.

As soon as her friends spotted her against the wall, they breathed a sigh of relief and nonchalantly glanced away, as if they had merely come outside for a breath of fresh air themselves.

"Don't worry, ladies." Justin's deep timbre vibrated through Kara's system as he gently grasped her chin in one hand and brought her gaze back to his, inches separating their eyes. He never once looked over his shoulder in the direction of her friends, but somehow he knew they were there. His warm delicious breath blew across her face as he continued. "I wasn't going to kidnap her. It was a bet, right? I think she won." The smile creeping across Justin's face was incredibly sexy.

Kara melted beneath his intense stare. She opened her mouth to speak, but no words came out.

"Just give us a minute, will you? And I promise to hand her over in one piece." Justin closed the gap to Kara's open mouth and covered it again, slower this time, with his own.

A giggle broke from the peanut gallery, but quickly faded from Kara's consciousness as all her attention once again diverted to the soft, warm, moist kiss taking over her senses.

Kara's body relaxed against Justin's, leaning into him in its traitorous mission to get closer. His left hand continued to hold her jaw, tenderly tilting her face to the side to get a better angle on her mouth. His right hand remained poised against the bare skin of her abdomen, gently grazing back and forth in silent torture. A knot of heat balled in Kara's stomach, creating an aching desire for him to inch those bold fingers lower until they cupped her sex with enough pressure to ease the need overwhelming her.

A groan vibrated in the night, jarring Kara back to her senses. Chuckling resumed a few feet to her right.

Oh my God, Kara. What are you doing? You don't even know this man you're allowing to paw you wantonly against the side of the building, making a spectacle of yourself for everyone in the parking lot.

Before Kara could act, Justin released her lips and leaned his forehead against hers again. He breathed heavily, a sexy grin turning up the corners of his mouth just enough to bring out tiny dimples on each cheek.

Kara sucked in a breath at the mental image of nuzzling those dimples.

"We are so not done here," Justin mumbled against her mouth as he nibbled on her top lip.

"I—"

"Yeah, I know. You have to go with your friends, but Kara… This is… You are…" Justin nibbled his way around to her bottom lip and sucked it gently between his own for just a moment.

Kara released the breath she'd been holding. "I am what?"

"There are…" he continued, kissing his way over her sensitive cheeks, roaming toward her ear "…so many…things…"

A clearing cough broke the spell Justin was weaving, reminding Kara her friends were standing two feet away watching this scene unfold. Probably hearing his words, too.

"I have to, um, go," she managed to utter while her body screamed *"No."* What she really wanted was for him to press his erection against her. A need was boiling inside her that she never knew existed before this moment.

Suddenly, as if he were touching a burning coal, Justin released her and stepped back. He held his hands up in a pose of surrender before running them through his hair. The tousled locks fell across his forehead when he released them, creating a just-woke-up look. Kara found herself wanting to reach up and touch the rumpled curls.

She shook the image from her mind and just gazed into Justin's deep penetrating brown eyes. "I—"

"Yeah, you should go... I'll 'call' you tomorrow to confirm." He made air quotes and one corner of his mouth turned up at the cliché.

"You don't—" Kara started to tell him he didn't have her number, but he was backing away, smiling.

"Don't worry. I'll find you," he muttered. In a flash, he was gone, disappearing between several trucks in the parking lot, his footsteps no longer resonating against the gravel.

Kara blinked and stared into the empty space wondering if the entire thing had been an illusion.

"Man, oh man." Kara jerked her gaze to the voice on her right, reminded once again she was not alone. "He was in a hurry," continued Jessica.

"And he was *hot*." Lindsey had a smirk of jealousy spreading across her face. Her eyebrows rose to indicate she was impressed. "And here I thought you were such a goody two shoes. Huh."

"A very lazy goody two shoes for the next week I guess." Kara gave a smug laugh and crossed her arms over her chest in a challenging pose. Would they really hold to their end of the deal? Did it matter?

"Well... Who wants to go back inside? Double or nothing?" Jess motioned toward the door.

"Hell, no. I'm going home. I have some studying to do." Kara didn't give them a chance to respond before heading across the parking lot toward the car. A moment of hesitation had Kara looking around her with the odd sense someone was watching her. A slight chill moved up her spine and she trembled. The night was still, however. No one in sight. Just like that, the feeling vanished.

The crunch of boots hitting the gravel behind her indicated her friends were following on her heels. Thank God. She didn't know what she would have done if they insisted on going back inside. She couldn't bear to taint her perfect evening with anything else that could possibly happen in that establishment tonight.

CHAPTER 3

Justin made a mad dash for his truck. His dick was rock hard, and Kara's lingering scent muddled his mind. Never, in all his life, had he reacted to someone so strongly. Just as he was about to open the door to the cab, he paused, took a deep breath, and scanned the parking lot. The scent of another wolf was in the air. Not one he was familiar with. It was faint, but it was there, bringing chills down his arms and killing his erection on a dime. It wasn't unusual for another pack to have a member running in the woods surrounding this area, but something about this particular scent made his hackles rise.

I must be losing my mind. Justin grabbed the door handle and yanked it open. One last glance at his surroundings and he dove into the truck and headed out of the parking lot. Whoever it was, surely it was nothing.

Justin drove a bit too fast the three miles out of town to his farm. He needed to shift and go for a run to burn some of the sexual frustration. But first, he needed to talk to Trevor.

Thank God Kara's friends bounded out of the dance

hall when they had. He'd had to fight the urge to take her right there. Sex in the parking lot was not the way he pictured their first time together.

Kara was... Kara was nothing like any other woman he'd ever been with. She deserved respect. And she was a gymnast. What the hell did that entail exactly? Justin aimed to find out first thing tomorrow.

As he rounded the corner and sped up the driveway to the single-story, ranch-style home he shared with Trevor, his tires lost traction and spun out on the dirt entrance before the vehicle pulled to a stop. Thank God his truck had four-wheel drive and anti-lock brakes.

Lord, Justin, slow the fuck down. You're going to kill yourself.

He bounded from the cab and nearly jogged into the house. Darkness and silence met him at the door. Trevor must still be out running. There would be no avoiding him when he returned. Forgoing his own need to run, Justin decided to take the bull by the horns, grabbed a beer, and settled himself down at the kitchen table to await Trevor's return. There was no need for lights really. Justin's vision was just as good in the dark as in broad daylight, one of the perks of being a shapeshifter.

After a long swig of beer, Justin leaned back in the chair and stared up at the ceiling. *Yeah.* As if perhaps the answers to all his problems would suddenly appear there, because everything in his life had changed in an instant.

The initial anger he'd felt when Kara first walked into Boot Scooters disappeared the moment he'd laid eyes on her. Kara was destined for him, and therefore his attraction to her was undeniable. He wanted her badly—fast, soon, and often. He foresaw a lot of cold showers in his near future, unless he could somehow woo her quickly into his arms, his bed, and his life.

His dick thickened at the thought of her soft lips, her

tongue tangling with his, her hard body pressed into his against the brick wall of the bar. Justin blew out a breath and stiffened in his chair.

Trevor was going to be pissed. *Right? Why?* It wasn't like Justin could have controlled this situation. He didn't *choose* to find a mate tonight. It just happened. But he and Trevor had been best friends since kindergarten when Trevor's parents tragically died in a mysterious accident no one ever spoke about and Justin's parents had taken him in. The two had become fast pals, nearly inseparable, closer than brothers. More like twins. And the antics they had been involved in over the years landed them many times in the principal's office and caused Justin's parents to go "prematurely gray," according to his mother. Justin chuckled at the memories.

The problem was he and Trevor shared more than just a house. They shared women, and this new development was taking Justin right off the market. Their lifestyle was about to undergo an uninvited change. Justin dreaded telling his best friend and brother what had happened this evening. Hell, they owned the farm together. Would one of them have to move out? Which one? And where would they go? *Shit.*

The clock on the wall was the only noise breaking the silence, ticking away the minutes until Trevor returned.

Trevor ran full speed toward the house. He had covered miles and miles of land in an effort to blow off the week's steam, dashing between trees, jumping over streams, clawing at the ground. Something had made him stop dead in his tracks about an hour ago. He paused in his full-out run to lift his nose into the air and sniff the surroundings.

Nothing. Not one thing seemed out of place or unusual about the woods tonight. But still, a niggling in the back of his mind told him it was time to go home. The urge to find Justin and check in was driving him to dash toward home with all haste. Especially since their bond had diminished significantly in the last hour. Either Justin was blocking him for some reason or he was in trouble. Neither case made Trevor feel any better.

As he bounded into the last clearing surrounding the house, he had an innate sense something was…off. The ranch-style, brick home looked the same as always, sprawled out between the huge oak trees Trevor and Justin had insisted be left standing when they had the place built three years ago.

Justin's truck was in the driveway, but no lights were on. Had he gone to bed already? Why was he even home yet? Usually on a Friday night, Justin preferred to mingle. Check out the scene at Boot Scooters to catch a game of pool with other pack members. It was the one night the two of them usually spent apart, fulfilling their own separate urges.

Trevor paused at the back door and allowed the change to take place. Bones cracked, muscles shortened, hair receded and within moments, Trevor stood, naked as the day he was born in his human form, reaching for the doorknob.

As soon as he opened the door leading into the kitchen, he knew his instincts to return home were right. Standing in the doorway, the first emotion to filter through his system was awareness. Something warm crawled beneath his skin. Fury followed close behind.

"Fuck." He glared at his best friend of twenty some-odd years and stomped into the room, not caring one iota that he had no clothes. The two of them had been naked together more times than he could count anyway, either changing forms or sharing women. Now was no different.

Justin's gaze met his, a look of uncertainty filling the depths of his deep brown eyes and furrowing his brow.

Trevor slammed the door to the kitchen behind him, causing Justin to jump in his seat.

"Why...do you...reek...of my... mate?" Red-hot anger surged through his veins. He couldn't breathe. Every muscle in his body froze tight. Fists at his sides, teeth gritted, he held back the urge to slam one of them into his best friend.

"Your...what?" Justin appeared totally confused. "Your...*your* mate?" He shook his head. "I can't believe this. So it's true." He smiled, getting to his feet.

What the hell is he talking about?

Trevor lifted his nose into the air and took a giant whiff, filling his lungs with the sweet feminine essence. Without a doubt the only smell in the room, besides that of Justin and himself, was definitely female—the woman he would spend the rest of his life with.

"Trevor, I—"

"Don't fucking 'Trevor' me. Did you know? Did you know she was mine before you put your grubby paws on her, sucked her tongue into your mouth? Tasted her neck?" The only thing stopping Trevor from changing back into his wolf form and attacking his best friend was the absence of the musky scent of sex.

Justin leaned his head back and roared in laughter. The action only infuriated Trevor more, making his shoulders tense in preparation for a fight.

"Thank you, God. And here I've been sitting for..." Justin glanced at the clock on the wall, "...thirteen minutes, dreading this confrontation more than anything in the world." He could barely spit the words out between his raucous chuckling.

"I don't know what you find so funny—" Trevor stepped closer to Justin, his hand curling into a fist. His face burned with anger.

"Trevor, stop." Justin's laughter died. His expression grew serious. "Sit." He pulled out a chair and headed for the fridge. As he returned with a pair of beer bottles, Trevor eyed him cautiously. "*Sit*," Justin repeated, angling the head of one bottle toward the chair with the air of authority that brooked no argument as he took a seat himself.

Trevor grabbed his jeans from the back of the chair and stepped into them, not bothering to zip them up. He dragging the legs across the wooden floor. "Fine, but you have some serious explaining to do." Trevor cautiously stared Justin in the eyes from across the table.

"I met a woman tonight," Justin began.

"*A* woman? No shit, Sherlock—"

"*Trevor*," Justin nearly shouted, "shut the fuck up for a minute and listen to me." He wasn't laughing anymore. Taking a sip of beer, he cleared his throat. "Like I said, I met her at Boot Scooters tonight. And, for your information, she is most assuredly *my* mate..." Justin paused before adding, "too." Justin stopped speaking and stared at Trevor.

Trevor let Justin's words seep into his muddled brain. "Your...*your* mate too?"

Was this a joke?

It was so uncommon. It had been years since two wolves bonded with the same female.

All their lives, he and Justin had shared women, always knowing one day it would come to an end when one of them met their mate, not taking seriously the possibility that perhaps, just maybe, fate would bless them with the fortunate ability to share the same mate.

"Well fuck me." Trevor sat back in the chair, relief washing over him. His best pal in the world had not stolen his mate. In fact, he had not taken her at all yet. A slow smile grew across his face and he slammed his hand down on the table. "I don't believe it. How did you know?"

"I didn't, until you walked through the door ready to pounce." He shook his head in disbelief. "No wonder I sensed such a strong vibe you were going to be ticked off." Justin laughed again and tipped his head back to take a long slow swallow of beer.

Without warning, Trevor's emotion changed from anger to jealousy and he didn't like the sudden resentment one bit. "What...what is she like?" he managed to say, amid visions of Justin frolicking around the dance hall with the woman they would spend the rest of their lives with.

Trevor had missed the entire episode and it stung like a sonofabitch.

"She's glorious. A tiny little pixie of a woman, about twenty-one years old, I think. Dainty, long, curly blonde hair, blue eyes like the ocean." Justin took a deep breath and exhaled it in a sigh while Trevor soaked in his every word.

"My hands spanned her entire waist she's so small. Barely five feet. She smells like honeysuckle and tastes like —" Justin jumped to attention. "Buddy, I was so fucking worried about you...us...she and I...you and I...she and you...*fuck*. You know what I mean. I thought it was the end of us. I mean I had hoped, but who knew?" Justin was rambling so fast Trevor barely grasped what the hell he was saying.

"So, when do I get to meet her? What did you tell her? What time are we seeing her tomorrow?" Trevor hesitated and stared at Justin. "Please tell me you fucking arranged something for tomorrow."

"Well, not exactly… And there's another matter… She's…human. And…a gymnast."

"A what? Are you talking about a flying through the air, flipping around, risking her neck kind of gymnast?" Trevor leaned forward, ready to pounce, as if Justin were to blame for this new piece of information.

Justin merely smiled and nodded. "You got it. That's the kind."

"Well, did you tell her to stop it? Did you tell her…? No," Trevor slammed his palm into his forehead, "of course you didn't. You didn't tell her any such thing, did you?"

Justin just continued to smile, tilted his head to one side, and crossed his arms over his chest, waiting on the futility of Trevor's words to dawn on him.

"Right. Well, what do we do now?" Trevor shook with the need to meet her, touch her, brand her as his. *Theirs.* His cock thickened with the thought of holding her. His blood was boiling.

"*We* don't do anything yet. *I* am meeting her for dinner tomorrow night. *You* can't be there." Justin's voice was beginning to irritate Trevor.

"Uh uh. No fucking way you get to have her all to yourself. That's just—"

"Trevor, she's a human. And rather inexperienced if my guess is correct. I could smell the innocence. It's been a while since she was with anyone. And I'm sure she hasn't ever pondered a ménage. And that doesn't take into consideration the fact we're wolves. We can't just pounce on her together like this. We have to take our time, weigh our options, lure her in slowly. In essence, court her."

Trevor heard the reason in Justin's voice but hated it all the same. A frustrated growl vibrated his throat.

"Unfortunately I met her first, so I have to be the one to get her to see the logic of our ways."

Shit. Justin was right. There was no other way. A deflated sensation caused Trevor to slump. Mating with a human was always dicey, even under the best of circumstances. They would completely freak her out if they descended on her like...a pack of wolves.

"Fine. But, I don't like it. And, Justin, you'd better be goddamn quick about it, because I swear, I won't be able to take it very long."

That was an understatement. Trevor leaped from his chair and headed straight for his end of the house. Thank God they each had their own master suite with adjoining bathroom, because frankly, he needed a long cold shower and time alone to lick his wounded ego.

Barry Welsh stood staring out his apartment window, fists gripped at his sides. His reflection stared back at him. *Fury.* His black hair stood in a disarray of spikes all over his head from running his hands through it. How had this happened?

The evening had started out just fine, better than fine actually. The hottest little number he ever laid eyes on had chosen this evening to come to Boot Scooters. He had nearly salivated watching her get out of the car with her friends. He could smell her sweet scent from the tree line, and his dick grew hard watching her through his binoculars as she kicked her boots in the gravel. She was *sweet*. A perfect diversion. He knew immediately she would be his.

And then that son of a bitch Justin dared to lay his hands on her.

He was still seething at the visual of *his* woman pressed up against the wall of that country bar like some common slut, the *bastard* groping her. Thank God he'd stuck to the tree line far away from the bar, preventing the asshole from readily noticing his scent and blowing his cover. Too bad the scene he'd witnessed through his high-power binoculars was now permanently etched in his mind. What could she possibly have seen in Justin, of all "people"?

For years Barry had put his own life on hold. Waiting. Watching. Looking for just the right opportunity.

It was time to move forward with his plans… *In fact,* he thought, as a slow sinister smile spread across his face, *even better*. The kind of pain he intended to inflict on his victim would be even sweeter. Everything had changed. Plan A just got an amendment.

CHAPTER 4

After rising earlier than usual to take care of the Saturday morning chores, Justin spent several hours Googling gymnastics and everything he could find about one Ms. Kara Shepherd. Trevor breathing down his neck the entire time made the search take longer than it should have.

"What's she like? What did she say? Where does she live? Details, man. I need details." Trevor paced the room behind Justin's chair.

"Calm down." He swiveled around to face a very frustrated Trevor. He honestly felt sorry for his friend's plight. "She's tiny. I mean really small. Barely comes up to here on me." He indicated a spot on his upper chest.

"Lord. How are we going to...? I mean..."

Justin chuckled, knowing what his buddy was alluding to. "I don't know, but we'll manage. Everyone does." He paused, looking toward Trevor before he continued. "She has the most angelic face. And her scent...it's intoxicating."

"This is crazy." Trevor ran his hands through already messy blond hair, making it stick up in spikes. "How are we...*you*...going to convince her she's ours?"

"I don't know, man. I honestly don't know. One step at a time." Justin took a deep breath. "First, I'm going to have dinner with her and get to know her better. I don't want to scare her. I'll just have to take it one step at a time."

"I have to go with you. I'll, you know, go to the bar or something. Just watch from there."

"No way. You'd never be able to do it. You'd pounce on her so fast, she'd run. You have to stay here and wait. Maybe she'll come back here with me."

"You're right, of course. I'd never last five minutes watching from the bar while you touched and sweet talked 'our' woman. Shit. I can't stand the...the waiting. It's killing me. I'm going to go for a run." Trevor marched right out the door, leaving Justin staring into space, his mind racing with the same thoughts.

No sooner had Trevor headed out than Ryan showed up unannounced. And he wasn't alone.

The second Justin heard the screen door to the kitchen swing open, he knew he was in trouble. The questions would go on and on for hours. His siblings were relentless when it came to mating.

"Justin? Where are you?"

"Coming." Justin dragged his sorry ass from the office and headed to meet the family in the kitchen.

"Justin..." Tessa was the first to greet him. Being the oldest and the only girl, she had always been rather motherly when it came to the boys. She pulled Justin into a hug and then held him back to look him in the eye. Only a few inches shorter than him, Tessa was a force to be reckoned with. Gorgeous, thick, dark wavy hair hung over her shoulders and eyes the same brown as his own stared into his. He felt younger than his twenty-eight years as she scrutinized him like a mother hen.

"What? Did you think I'd look different?" Justin chuckled and wiggled free of her grasp.

"Congrats." The others, Ryan, Charles, and Michael, stated practically in unison while alternately slugging him in the arm or giving him a pat on the back, each in his own style of affection.

Tessa brushed them aside. "So? Details, details. What's she like? When do we get to meet her? Oh, my God, I almost forgot! How did Trevor take the news?" His sister covered her mouth with one hand, shock registering.

"Well, that's interesting actually."

Tessa looked around. "Where *is* Trevor? Oh, my. Was he pissed? Did he leave?"

Justin laughed. "No. No. I don't think he'll be going anywhere. That's the best part. He's mated to Kara also." He waited for their reaction.

"Seriously? That's great. Did you bring her home with you last night? Was he here?" Tessa's questions were firing so fast, Justin didn't know which to answer first.

His brothers just leaned against the counter and the table. Everyone knew there was no trying to interrupt Tessa when she was on a role.

"Not hardly. She's a nice girl. I'm sure Ryan told you she's human." Justin took a seat. "It was tough, but I had to let her go with her friends. Believe me, Trevor almost pummeled me good when he got home and smelled her all over me. I've never been so relieved in my life."

"Wonderful. When are you seeing her again?" Tessa moved to the fridge and pulled out a soda. It was only ten thirty in the morning, but the whole family would have been up since before the crack of dawn tending to the family farm. Not too early for lunch and caffeine in most of their minds.

The rest of them all lived on his parents' land. Tessa had her own house with her husband and kids, but the younger brothers lived in the main house. Their parents had always been strict, but incredibly loving at the same time. No one had a great urge to leave the sprawling ranch-style home they'd grown up in. Justin had only moved out three years ago when he and Trevor decided to buy their own dairy farm.

"I'm taking her out tonight." *Which isn't soon enough.*

"When do we get to meet her?" Charles directed his question at Justin but then turned to Tessa when everyone froze. "What," he raised his eyebrows, "can't I ask a question or two also?"

"Ha, ha." Tessa cocked her hip out and put one hand on it. "No one's stopping you."

Justin wasn't about to share Kara with anyone besides Trevor yet. "Give us some time, guys. Trevor hasn't even met her yet. No one's meeting her until we ease her into our lifestyle. Remember, she has no idea we're shapeshifters, let alone that she's about to begin a life with two men."

Michael chuckled and reached into the fridge himself. "Don't you have any beer in here?"

"Get out of there. Even if I did, your underage self wouldn't be having any, and besides, it's not even noon." Justin moved to brush Michael aside and reached in to hand his twenty-year-old baby brother a cola.

"Mom is going to flip. She said to tell you to, and I quote, 'bring that sweet girl by the house ASAP.'" Ryan's voice was mocking the exact tone their mother assuredly used that morning.

Justin just grinned. "What did Dad say?" Of course

Ryan would've barged into the house last night and blared Justin's entire business through the imaginary loud speaker, Ryan's mouth.

Ryan continued, "Again, I quote, ''bout time.'"

"Figures." Their father was not known for wasting verbs and nouns.

"Of course that was before he knew you and Trevor were *both* going to mate with Kara." Ryan's grin reached ear to ear. "Not sure how he's going to respond to that tidbit of info."

Justin gritted his teeth. His parents had always been as understanding as any parents could have been regarding Justin's lifestyle. It was no secret, although unspoken, he and Trevor shared their women. It didn't mean they expected Justin and Trevor to form a permanent relationship with just one woman, however. It was rare, relatively unheard of.

As if Tessa had read Justin's thoughts, she spoke again. "I wonder when was the last time three wolves mated, not to mention two wolves with a human? I'm going to have to check that out."

"You do that, won't you?" Justin began. "And be sure to let Dad know when you figure it out. It will ease his mind a bit."

Not that his parents didn't adore Trevor. They had raised him as their own since the age of five, but that didn't mean they intended for Justin and him to mate with the same woman.

"Now, get out of here, all of you." Justin moved to shove them out the back door. "I have things to take care of."

Tessa laughed. "Riiight. I mean, you better get going on your shower and choose which jeans you're going to wear with those boots of yours. You've got, what…" she looked down at her watch, "…seven and a half hours before your date." With that she made a run for the door, Justin's brothers scrambling after her to avoid Justin's wrath.

By noon he had a headache, furrows etched into his forehead, and a frown molded in displeasure. Thank God Kara was about to graduate, because Justin didn't think he could stand to watch her flying through the air for very many weeks. It seemed like a terribly dangerous sport.

After lunch, Justin headed for the barn for some hard labor and then went for a long run. Even the time spent in wolf form didn't lessen his anxiety. The clock seemed to trickle at an interminably slow speed toward the six o'clock hour. He'd found her address and phone number easily on the Internet earlier, but when he called, no one answered. A brief message was all he left, confirming the location and time for this evening. He was almost relieved he hadn't had to stammer out a conversation over the phone with her. He just wanted her in his arms again.

Kara walked into the Steak House promptly at six. She was feeling a little uneasy about meeting Justin, a man she barely knew. On the other hand, her body's reaction to him had been undeniable. They clearly had chemistry. She couldn't resist the urge to see what her physical response might lead to. Butterflies refused to stop fluttering through her stomach at the idea of seeing him again, but what did she know about him really? That he liked to dance? That he could kiss? Man, oh man, could he kiss.

If she'd been home when he'd called her apartment earlier, she might have been tempted to cancel. Her nerves were getting the better of her. But, he hadn't left a number, and she couldn't bring herself to just not show up.

She hadn't been sure what to wear to this pseudo first date and almost left the apartment in jeans and a sweater. However, when Lindsey and Jessica saw her, they fussed about her appearance, causing her to end up in a rather short, black, formfitting dress, hugging her hips and barely covering her ass. She looked down at herself now and smoothed her hands over the wrinkles that had settled in her lap from the car ride. How had she let those two talk her into this outfit? Was it too sexy? She had felt confident and fantastic alone in the car, but now she was trying hard not to feel apprehensive. Taking a deep breath for courage, she reached her hands up to smooth back her hair. Usually she liked to straighten the long curls. It was easier to get a rubber band around the thick mass in the gym, but tonight Jess insisted she wear it down and natural. According to Jess, she looked "like an angel with all those natural blonde waves floating about."

She scanned the crowded restaurant filled with Saturday night diners.

"Hey there," came a low sultry voice from right behind her ear at the same time a possessive hand landed on her lower back. She shivered at the contact. Before she could turn her head completely in the direction of the voice, soft lips reached around to meet hers in a gentle greeting, warming her insides and sucking all reason from her system.

When his soft sexy lips retreated a few inches, she finally saw Justin, his deep chocolate gaze scanning her face, a broad smile lighting the room and making her feel at ease.

"Well, hello yourself, cowboy." Was the sensual voice she heard her own?

He looked very similar to last night—jeans, dusty cowboy boots clearly worn for more than just Friday night partying, a rust-colored western shirt stretched across his torso defining his strong muscular body to perfection. He looked…delicious. Warmth continued to spread through her body at his proximity.

Kara wanted him to continue the kissing part and skip the dinner part. *What the hell are you thinking? Since when do you fall so head over heels for a man?*

"You look fantastic." Justin scanned Kara's body appreciatively from head to toe and back up to her face. Perhaps she should have found the action insulting, but somehow he made her feel sexy. "I already have our table, right over here." He indicated the direction behind her with a nod of his head and a slight pressure on her back.

Justin angled Kara through the crowd of noisy patrons toward a cozy corner table for two, never removing his hand from her back, an intimacy she was acutely aware of.

Was he always this familiar on a first date?

A spike of envy stabbed Kara in the gut at the thought of Justin on other first dates.

Of course he's had other first dates, you dimwit. Hundreds, assuredly. Just look at him.

The man next to her was a Greek god, the god of cowboys if there would have been such a thing. She bet he would be fabulous posing nude for a class of art students. She literally shook at the image of him naked in front of a group of people.

Seriously Kara, you just met him. You don't own him.

"Kara? Is this all right?" How long had he been speaking to her? *Darn.*

"Of course. This is fine."

Justin, in a true gentlemanly fashion, pulled out Kara's chair and pushed her up close to the table as she sat.

"So, I hope you're hungry and you like steak." He paused to look at her. "You aren't a vegetarian, are you?"

"No, of course not. I love a good steak, occasionally."

Justin's warm, inviting smile made her feel at ease.

Kara smiled, thinking perhaps, just maybe, he actually wanted to impress *her*. She had been out of the dating scene for so long she didn't even remember what it felt like to be *wanted*. Well, to be honest, she had never really been *in* the dating scene, not much anyway. And she was rarely dressed in more than a leotard and sweatpants, with her hair pulled up in a ponytail, never considering attracting anyone's attention.

It felt fantastic to sit back and relax, let her hair down, literally, and enjoy the...flat-out stare coming from the other side of the table.

"Occasionally?" He leaned toward her across the small table, grinning. She clamped her legs together underneath the table to keep them from bouncing up and down in a nervous dance. A habit she had yet to break.

"Well..."

"I'm just teasing. Just wanted to make sure you weren't going to order a small side salad and sit there pretending ladies don't actually 'eat.'" His smile was infectious.

"Oh, I eat. That's for sure. Probably more than any other woman you've ever dated. Unless you've had the occasion to date other athletes who spend hours a day in a gym working off calories at a rate faster than they can be consumed." Kara found herself leaning forward. She fingered the menu in front of her without actually glancing at it.

Justin reached across the table and took Kara's hand in his own in a gesture that seemed as natural as walking. "Can't say that I have." He glanced down to peruse the menu, but his thumb was caressing her palm in such a distracting manner she couldn't think, let alone read. She never took her eyes off him, just continued staring at the top of his head while intermittently glancing at their entwined hands. Heat ran up her arm.

"Can I get you two something to drink? An appetizer perhaps?" Kara started a bit at the interruption and turned to face the waitress. She was a bubbly little brunette with short spiked hair, apparently the style for the sixteen-ish crowd lately. The only problem was "Gina," as her nametag indicated, was looking only at Justin. Drooling actually.

Justin didn't seem to notice. In fact, he didn't even look directly at the girl when he spoke. "I'll have a Budweiser. Kara? Wait… Let me guess, mineral water?"

Ooh, he's good. Impressive.

Kara smiled and turned to "Gina," though she could have refrained from making the polite gesture for all the waitress knew. "Yes, thank you. Mineral water for me."

As the teenager backed away from the table, continuing to watch Justin, she ran straight into a busboy who had to wobble his tray of precariously stacked dirty dishes back and forth to avoid dumping the entire lot on the floor. Gina snapped around to apologize and then darted off in search of their drinks.

"So…tell me about yourself." Justin's voice pulled Kara's gaze back in his direction. She wasn't at all sure he even knew if the server had been male or female. A new warmth flowed through her. He made her feel incredibly sexy. She could barely concentrate. *His fingers are running patterns over the back of my hand…*

"Well, I'm from Portland. My parents still live there. Only child."

"That's nice. To be so close to your family. Do you go home often?"

It was difficult to answer all Justin's inquiries with his

thumb rubbing against her palm driving her to distraction and his intense stare just a few scant inches from her face across the small table. What she really wanted to do was tune out the rest of the world and lean in for another of his fantastic kisses. The thought caught her off guard.

Why on earth was she so drawn to him? Almost as if they'd always been together. As though they always would be...

"No, I don't go home too often anymore. I'm too busy studying and working at the gym. My parents usually come to my meets though."

"I'm looking forward to seeing you myself. When do I get a preview?"

"Well, technically anytime I guess. It wouldn't be very interesting, but anyone is welcome to come to practices. My last official meet is next Saturday. And it happens to be a home competition, so you can always come to that... If you really want to." It warmed her heart that he seemed interested in her gymnastics career.

"I can't wait."

"Here you go..." A voice to Justin's side interrupted the bubble he and Kara were living in. A familiar high-pitched youthful tone, must have been the waitress. Justin glanced over his shoulder as she stepped aside and a tall slender man set drinks in front of Justin. "Are you ready to order?" the waitress asked as the bartender walked away.

Order? *Oh, shit, right. Steak restaurant. It is customary to order a meal when dining out.*

Justin jerked his attention to the menu in front of him, scanned the page and silently chose a nice steak. Then he looked over the top of the menu. "Kara? Do you know what you want?"

Her perfect little bow mouth, her beautiful curls bouncing around in an unruly fashion no matter how many times she reached to tuck them behind her ears sent his mind reeling. *Sexy.* He couldn't bring himself to release the hold he had on her hand. So dainty and feminine.

"I'll have the filet mignon, medium, and a baked potato, butter only, please."

Justin smiled his approval.

"And you, sir?" Now he felt downright old. Glancing at the waitress, he assessed her to be in her teens. No wonder.

"I'll have the T-bone, medium rare, and a loaded baked potato."

"All right. Would either of you like a salad to start with? We have a house salad just right for two. If you'd like to share."

"Sounds good to me. Kara?" Justin returned his gaze to her upturned face.

"Sure. Perfect." She smiled sweetly at the waitress.

"I'll get your order in right away." The girl leaned a little closer than strictly necessary to remove the menu Justin was holding.

Was she flirting with him? *Seriously?*

He shivered at the thought. She was a child. Almost half his age.

"So, what do you do for fun?" he asked as the waitress walked away. Justin wanted to know everything there was to know about Kara. Besides personal interest, Trevor would absolutely kill him if he didn't extract serious details.

Trevor.

Justin had left the man pacing the floors of their home in frustration. He begged Justin to at least let him come along and sit discreetly at the bar, but Justin knew Trevor all too well. No way in hell could he have managed to stay out of range and not pounce this lovely mate of theirs.

Kara chuckled, a soft little tinkling sound that reached in and squeezed Justin's heartstrings. "Fun? I hate to break this to you, but the sum total of the fun I've had in the last four years occurred against the outside wall of a country bar...last night."

Fuck. Justin's balls tightened at the thought of having been the only man to touch her in recent memory.

"You...really? Don't you go out with your friends? Frat parties? Night clubs? Dates?"

"Not really. Well...no. I haven't had time, and I guess I haven't really cared. Before...now..." This last bit she half mumbled, her head angled to the side, her smile making Justin shift in his seat to make room for his growing erection.

"Well then, my little pixie, I guess I better make sure you have the time of your life tonight, especially if the only other evening you have to compare it to is last night. I'm pretty sure I can top it without much effort." Justin winked at her. He wasn't sure if he felt more elated by the privilege of her presence or flat out scared shitless from being presented with the task of showing her a good time.

Her soft giggle erupted again. "You're doing a fine job so far. So, what do you do? You said you work on a farm?"

"Yes, I live just out of town on a dairy farm...with my long-time friend Trevor." Might as well throw his name out there so she could start getting used to it.

"A dairy farm? Sounds like a lot of work. I've never actually been close to a cow before."

Justin smiled at her honesty. *You're about to be. And what about wolves? Have you been close to a wolf before?*

Kara was in for a shock when she discovered the extent

of Justin's and Trevor's lives. Besides owning and operating the large dairy farm, the two had several other pack members on their staff. Not to mention the conglomeration of other farms in the area owned and operated by family and friends. It was a giant Mecca keeping the shapeshifters out of the public eye and giving them the space they needed to roam free whenever they desired. Cows never told a soul about the wolves sometimes used to herd them across the land. Downright convenient at times.

"It's not really complicated. Cows are easy to get along with and everyone needs milk."

"Hmm. Living in this area, I've always wondered what a working dairy farm was like."

Justin squeezed her hand, leaned forward to grasp her other hand, and pulled her sweet endearing face toward his. "Honey, you can come check it out any time you want. My door is always open." *You have no idea how wide open the door is, nor how satisfied you'll be after you come in.*

Justin closed the last few inches between them for a long tender kiss. When he finally pulled back, Kara was breathing heavily, clearly as aroused as he was. Her cheeks were red. Her lips looked luxuriously well-kissed, wet, swollen.

A throat clearing to the side of them broke the spell.

"Your salad?" The waitress phrased it like a question. As though she were interrupting something quite a bit more important than sustenance and wasn't entirely sure they would appreciate it. And she wasn't too far off the mark. If Justin weren't so hungry, he might have just grabbed Kara and headed for the truck.

Instead, he leaned back, released his grip on Kara's hands, breaking physical contact with her for the first time that evening, regretting the loss of her warmth and spark immediately. His gaze never strayed from hers though, and they seemed to be in a staring match.

Plates appeared in front of them, a large salad in the center of the table.

"May I?" Thank goodness the waitress took the liberty of filling their plates, because Justin didn't relish the idea of fumbling around with the salad tongs, dropping lettuce all over the table.

"Thank you," Kara graciously replied.

When the girl finished serving them and wandered away, Kara reached for her fork. "I'm starving. This looks delicious."

"Yes, it does." Fortunately Kara glanced down at her plate to spear a vegetable and didn't catch Justin staring at her lips. When she wrapped those lips around the mouthful and then reached her tongue out to lick a dab of salad dressing from the corner of her mouth, Justin nearly moaned. He couldn't wait to feel those lips wrapped around his cock. He had to discreetly reach under the table and adjust his growing erection.

"Are you going to eat?" Kara inquired with a giant grin. "Or simply watch me eat?"

Busted.

Slowly breaking himself from the spell she held him under, he swallowed. "I guess I could join you, but it was so much better just watching you enjoy yourself." He doubted he would taste a thing.

Justin reached for his own fork and knife and tackled the lettuce without really seeing it. Who cared about salad right now?

Soon the delicious aroma of prime steak wafted up to Justin's nose, tantalizing his senses, as the waitress removed the salad plates and replaced them with the main course.

Kara looked down. "This looks and smells delicious. I can't remember the last time I had a filet." She reached for the utensils, cut a small bite, and placed it in her mouth. God, how Justin wished he were the tines of the fork. How could eating a steak seem so erotic? Kara even closed her eyes to savor the morsel…and moaned.

Thank God Justin was so dark-complected, otherwise he would surely appear beet red at the orgasmic experience before him. He struggled to pay attention to his own meal, glancing up frequently, unable to keep his gaze from Kara's face. He couldn't believe he was sitting across the table from the woman he would spend his entire life with, the woman whose body he and Trevor would worship. He couldn't wait until the two of them made her scream in ecstasy. If she were half as responsive in bed as she was to a steak meal, she would be the death of him.

"You don't get out much if this is the reaction you have to a steak. Or…perhaps you have this reaction to every meal."

It wasn't really a question, but Justin raised one eyebrow to indicate he was intrigued.

"Well, there's only one way for you to find out."

Damn, she was so hot when she flirted with him like that. She had no idea how many meals she was going to share with him in the near future. Visions of him and Trevor feeding her, blindfolded and trussed to their bed, scampered through his mind. Sweat built up on his forehead and it had nothing to do with the heat of the restaurant.

Kara shook her long curls back from her face and took another bite.

"Do you always drink water? I could order a bottle of wine or something if you'd like?" Surely mineral water wasn't the only thing she ever imbibed.

"No, not always. I enjoy a glass of wine from time to time, but it's just easier when I'm in the middle of the season to not drink at all. I get so dehydrated the next day."

That made sense. Good to know she would be completely in charge of her faculties when he eventually sprung how they were going to spend the rest of their lives together and with another man as well. Justin tensed at the thought of telling her anything. This was surely not how she would have pictured her life veering after graduation.

The pleasant silence between them while they ate was not uncomfortable. They fell into a rhythm. It shouldn't have surprised Justin. After all, he'd heard how it would be when you found your mate.

Finally Kara leaned back in her seat. "I'm stuffed. How did I actually eat all of it?"

True enough, her plate was nearly empty.

"Shall we go for a walk? It's nice outside." *Please say yes.*

"That sounds lovely."

Justin quickly assessed the bill which had miraculously appeared at his elbow at some point, left some twenties and stood to reach for Kara's hand.

Hot. It was the only word Kara could think of to describe the intensity of the evening. As soon as the two of them walked outside, she immediately felt the relief of the cool evening air blowing against her skin. It was barely May, so the evenings were still quite chilly.

Justin took her hand and began walking aimlessly down the street.

"We have a mock practice meet tomorrow morning if you're really interested in seeing me perform." Kara let the statement hang in the air, holding her breath. She had no idea why his reaction was so important to her, but she did know she wanted this man to care, really *care*—about her and what mattered to her.

Justin turned to look her in the eye with a genuine smile, stopping them on the sidewalk. "I'd love that. What time?"

Kara released the breath she was holding with a soft whoosh. "Ten. If that's too early on a Sunday for you, I understand. You don't have to get there promptly or anything. Just wander in whenever you want."

Justin chuckled. "I work on a farm. Believe me, I've had two meals by ten."

"Oh, sure. Right." Kara couldn't take her eyes off Justin's face. He was so full of life. So...genuine. They stood like statues in the middle of the sidewalk, the only movement her unruly hair; suddenly it blew from behind to obstruct her fantastic view.

Before Kara could reach up to tame the meandering curls, Justin's hands were on her face. He gently pushed the crazy mop back and held it in place behind her head while he leaned in to take possession of her mouth for the third time that evening.

Heat erupted in Kara's cheeks even before he made contact with her lips. The kiss was so gentle, soft.

"Mmm… I could kiss you all night long," he mumbled against her mouth. "Your lips are delicious."

The heat unfurling in Kara's cheeks spread down the front of her to tighten her chest. Her breasts felt suddenly too large for the small lace bra she wore. She ached to have him run his hands down her body.

"It's early still. Would you like to come back to the farm and meet your first cow?" Justin grinned at her.

Yes. But… What should she say? They only met yesterday. One hot, sweltering kiss against a wall, dinner, followed by another steaming mouth-to-mouth session on the sidewalk. Wasn't it a bit too soon to go back to "his place"? Wouldn't he expect too much of her? And...to be honest, wouldn't she be powerless to stop him?

He must have sensed her unease because he quickly spoke again. "I didn't mean to put you on the spot. I swear I didn't mean to insinuate we would... That I would... What I'm trying to say is, I just thought you might like to see the farm, hang out a bit. I promise to return you to your place early. I know you have a busy day tomorrow. My roommate, Trevor, is there. I'd like you to meet him. He's a good guy. You two will get along great."

His roommate? How much trouble could she get into if his roommate was home? Sounded safe enough. And the dairy farm would be very interesting. A totally different life from the one she'd known.

Justin leaned his forehead against Kara's. "We can do it another time if it makes you uncomfortable. Want to go to a movie or something? It's still early."

"No. No. That's fine. I would love to see the farm."

Justin just smiled brightly at her acquiescence and turned to tug her back down the sidewalk the way they'd come. "Well then, let's go see some cows."

Kara felt incredibly comfortable with Justin. Something just felt...right.

CHAPTER 5

"You live here?" Kara stared out the window of Justin's truck at the acres and acres of green pastures surrounding the rustic ranch house. It was almost dark, but she could still make out the buildings and vehicles. A large red barn set off to the side, a dusty green tractor parked outside. She had no idea people still owned and ran individual farms.

"Well, yes. Where else would I live?" Oh, so he was amused by her reaction.

"Funny. You might not have mentioned that the place was so…big. This place is massive." Kara stared out at the "home" Justin lived in, unable to close her mouth. Justin pulled into a circular driveway to park just outside the front doors.

"I'm glad you like it."

Kara was barely aware of Justin exiting the truck. Before she could blink, he opened her door and reached for her hand.

"Would you like to come *inside* the house, or are you good just standing here in the driveway." Justin was laughing softly when she finally brought herself to look away from the wrap-around front porch that was the focal point surrounded by burgundy bricks. A porch swing even creaked softly in the breeze.

"Justin? Why do I get the feeling you *own* this place?"

"Umm, of course." He looked at her quizzically. "What did you think?"

"You said you *worked* on a farm. I...I was picturing pastures, milking or...or, something." *Shit. Literally. I was picturing grunt work.* Kara bit her bottom lip to avoid sticking her foot any further into her mouth.

Luckily Justin just laughed harder. "Sorry to disappoint you, sweetheart. Trevor and I own the farm. We have for about three years. It's hard work sometimes, but business has been good, and we've really enjoyed it."

Justin grabbed Kara's forearm and let his fingers slide down until he had a hold of her hand. Goosebumps erupted all over her skin at the gentle and increasingly familiar contact. He was almost constantly touching her in some way. Perhaps it should have seemed too personal, possessive, but coming from him it just seemed...perfect. She actually loved his continual contact.

Justin tugged on Kara's hand and motioned toward the house with his head. "Come on. I want you to meet Trevor."

He quickly swept her through the front door into an enormous family room. The area was so...warm. Welcoming.

The lived-in feeling of the self-proclaimed bachelor pad struck her immediately. A large sectional sofa formed a giant U-shape in the center of the room in a pattern of rust and browns. The area rug extending from the couch was a luxurious shaggy beige. Kara found herself wanting to take her shoes off and sink her feet into the tall pile.

"What do you think?" Justin's voice was surprisingly eager.

Kara glanced at him to see an expression of hope staring back at her. He seemed to be holding his breath as though it mattered a great deal to him that she liked his home.

"It's wonderful, Justin. I just love it."

What was not to love?

A soft shade of brown covered the walls and met up with hardwood floors. Pillows in a variety of autumn colors were strewn around the sofa and in front of it, begging someone to lie on the carpet and relax in front of the enormous flat-screen TV or listen to the stereo system filling the built-in, wall-to-ceiling shelves.

"Would you like something to drink?" Justin continued to pull Kara through the living area and into the largest kitchen she'd ever seen. Clean. Modern. Sleek. Weird. *How do a couple of bachelors keep their kitchen so tidy?* "I don't have mineral water, but..." He pointed to the sink and faucet, teasing her.

"Ha ha. I'm fine."

Kara stared at Justin as he gathered her into his embrace. He lowered his mouth to hers in another mind-boggling kiss, taking her breath away.

A sudden noise to Kara's left made her jump and spin in the direction of a screen door to the backyard banging closed. Heat suffused her face at having been caught kissing.

Standing in the doorway, gasping for air, was the second perfect male specimen Kara had met in two days. His blond hair was darker than hers, wavy, and hung across his forehead, disheveled. He seemed to have run to the house. Emerald eyes stared at her...trapped her. A shiver ran through Kara's entire body. Had they met before? She had the oddest sensation she should know him. Then again, she'd felt the same reaction with Justin last night. How peculiar. Incredibly strange.

What the hell is wrong with you, Kara?

When she licked her lips, tasting Justin's kiss, her senses returned slowly. Her mouth felt suddenly dry. Her heart beat rapidly.

She realized she had turned in Justin's arms to face away from him and still stood in his embrace, staring like a madwoman at his friend. His roommate, for Christ's sake.

"Kara, this is Trevor." Justin pulled Kara tighter against his chest, his arms wrapped around her almost stiffly. She leaned back against him. And prayed whatever freaky part of nature screaming at her to get a taste of Trevor too, would pass. Quickly.

"Hi." Trevor approached Kara slowly. His swagger was hesitant. Sexy.

Stop it.

She could not rein in her thoughts. He was at least as big as Justin. Built. Did the two of them spend the entire day working out? Did steroids fill the water out here? Surely even the physical labor of a farm wouldn't be enough to turn ordinary men into mouthwatering gods.

As he got closer, Kara tensed. His gaze narrowed in on her, wandered over her entire body like a predator. When he finally arrived to within a foot of her, he stopped. Kara froze in her position tucked under Justin's chin.

Trevor reached for Kara's hand. "Nice to meet you. I've heard...well, not much actually."

Kara tentatively took Trevor's hand. Sparks raced up her arm. The electricity shooting between them muddled her mind on so many levels.

What the hell is going on here?

With his free hand, Trevor reached for Kara's forearm,

the endearing gesture only managing to add to Kara's confusion over her seemingly emotional instability. He, too, had an affinity for touching as much of her skin as possible, even for this simple gesture of greeting. She was acutely aware of both men's possessive hands wrapped around her arm, her fingers, her stomach…and she wanted them to. In fact, she wanted more.

How could she possibly be this attracted to two men?

She desperately wanted Trevor to lean in closer. His scent was as arousing to her as Justin's. Distinct, but equally masculine. Woodsy.

"Nice to meet you, too." The greeting sounded tight and high-pitched to her ears. Trevor stood incredibly close to Kara, but Justin didn't seem to notice, or care.

"How was dinner?" Trevor stepped back and released his gentle hold on Kara's arm and hand. Immediately she felt the loss of his heat, his energy, but not the attraction.

"It was great," Justin responded.

Thank God, because Kara didn't really think she could speak again without squeaking. Embarrassment at her strange erratic behavior flooded her and she felt the same flush rise to her cheeks that always managed to give her away.

"I promised Kara some cows," Justin continued.

"Cows?" A perplexed look came over Trevor's rugged face, a slight chuckle escaping from between his lips, one side of his mouth reaching up in a half smile. His gaze never left hers.

Kara wanted to touch his skin, feel the smooth angles of his jaw against the back of her hand. Not for the first time, she shivered.

"I've never…" *Well, that was articulate.*

"She hasn't seen cows up close before. I figured we could remedy that."

"Well, then. Let's head to the barn. I think I can muster up a few cows easily enough."

His sexy smile must be a Trevor trademark.

Kara wanted to taste his lips at least as much as she had wanted to devour Justin's just moments ago. When she glanced up at Justin, instead of jealousy, Kara thought she saw...relief?

Justin released his possessive hold on her just enough to take her right hand and begin pulling her toward the back door Trevor had just come through. Thank goodness, because if he let go she'd probably trip over her own two feet, refusing to get with the program.

"Are you coming, Trevor? Trevor? The cows?" Trevor could hear Justin's words ringing silently in his head but could not yank his attention from Kara. He'd merely spun slowly around as Justin dragged her through the kitchen. The magnetic energy was palpable. Could she feel it? Of course she could. He could smell her arousal. He'd seen her squeeze her thighs together when he reached for her.

"Man, put your tongue back in your mouth. You look like a cub standing there. You're going to scare her off before we even have her." Justin looked impatient as Trevor finally glanced up into his face.

The two of them had been able to communicate telepathically for as long as they had been friends. Not all wolves possessed the ability, but certain ones had a special affinity. Especially bonded wolves, husbands and wives. Perhaps they had always been destined to bond with each other in a mating with one shared woman, which explained the special ability to converse without speaking.

"Cows. Right." Trevor followed behind Kara out the

door, the proximity of her body in front of his an ever-present thought. He had to grip his hands into fists at his sides to keep from reaching out to touch her. Justin had run his hands down her arms and now held her fingers in his. The contact he had with her was going to drive Trevor bonkers before he got to have his turn. *"Can you...I don't know...touch her a little less? You're killing me."*

Justin's laugh rang into Trevor's head, audible only to him. *"You'll get your turn, and then some."*

The short walk to the barn behind the house was silent. For Kara at least. Had the barn moved farther away from the house than it had been just moments ago? He could see it perfectly well in the evening shadows, but Kara would be ambling blindly toward the red frame ahead.

Trevor was completely unable to control the increasing level of desire consuming his body. He stared at Kara's fine ass as she swayed in front of him. The tight fit of her dress defined the muscular globes that would nestle perfectly against Trevor when he took her from behind. Thank God he brought up the rear because he had to adjust his growing hard on several times behind the confines of his jeans.

"You didn't mention she was so...fucking hot." Trevor didn't take his gaze from Kara's butt.

"Oh, I'm sure I did. You just weren't listening."

By the time they entered the barn, the cool evening air had grown warmer. *"Is it hot out here?"*

Silent laughter was the only response from Justin.

When the three of them reached the first stall and leaned over the gate, Trevor could see Kara was definitely fidgeting. She was as attracted to the two of them as they were to her. The concept would be foreign to her. Unheard of. She attempted to focus on the gigantic animal inside the stall, but her shifting gaze told him she centered her awareness on the men. Justin, on her right, wrapped a possessive hand around her shoulder and grasped the fence on the other side. Trevor stood incredibly close to her on her left, allowing his biceps to rub against hers, creating an electric current between the three of them.

"This is Bessy," Justin began, his voice completely calm as though not one strange thing was wrong with the universe. "She's our oldest. Retired. We're rather attached to her, so we kept her. She lives a life of luxury here on the farm." Justin chuckled and reached his right hand into the stall, making a smacking noise with his mouth, luring the tame animal over to receive a pet.

"You can touch her if you'd like. She won't bite."

But I might. Trevor looked over his shoulder at Kara's face, just inches away. So close he could feel the heat of her exhale against his face as she turned toward him.

She kept licking her lips. It drove Trevor mad. He wanted to lean just those last few inches and trail his own tongue over her ripe pink mouth. *"Dude, her tongue is...is..."*

"I know. Maddening, isn't it? Wait 'til she wraps it around yours," Justin teased.

Kara yanked her gaze toward the cow. Did she think staring at the large mammal would dampen the emotional charge? *Not.* She shuffled her feet and Trevor glanced down to her legs which she clenched tightly together. He couldn't help the smile spreading across his face. She was aroused. Undeniably. He could smell it in the air.

Justin described the cow, what type she was, how much she weighed, how long they'd had her. On and on. Trevor knew his pal was buying time. Giving Kara the opportunity to get comfortable in their presence. Justin's grip on the wooden fence tightened in an effort to keep himself from reaching under her dress and feeling the results of her excitement with his palm. *Too soon.*

"So, Justin tells me you're a gymnast," Trevor finally managed to direct the comment at her. *"Man, she's so aroused. And she has no idea what to do about it. Can you smell it on her?"*

"Of course I can. Why do you think I'm spending so much time talking about fucking cows? Thought it might take my mind off the hard on threatening to explode in my jeans here."

Justin was nothing if not eloquent.

"I am. Well for another week anyway." Kara tipped her chin up in Trevor's direction once again, her eyes locking with his. "I'm too old…for the sport, that is. My days are numbered." Her smile was so lovely. Dimples broke out on both cheeks. Trevor wanted to nibble around them. And he would. Later.

"I'd hardly consider you old." Here he was thinking of all the ways to thoroughly debauch this woman and worrying about how inexperienced she was for the sexual ideas running through his mind.

"By gymnastics standards," Kara continued. "I'll probably never leave the sport completely, but my competitive days are just about over."

"It sounds very…um, dangerous. Isn't it?" *Great, Trevor. You sound like her dad.*

Kara laughed, a sweet light sound tinkling in the air, sending a chill down Trevor's arms. "I guess. I never really think about it anymore."

"Hmm." No way was he going to be able to support the idea of her continuing on this deadly path. *"When are you planning to tell her this gymnastics gig is not going to work for us?"*

"Ha ha. Just after you do." Oh, so Justin was pawning the problem off on the current third wheel. *"Besides, you heard her. It's only for another week."*

Trevor watched as Kara squirmed against Justin's chest

firmly pressed to her back. With both men crowding her, they had to be invading her personal space. It wasn't dampening her lust any. Her scent permeated the air between them. What would it feel like to be skin to skin with her? To have both him and Justin sandwiched against her naked body?

"I should go," she blurted out, intruding on Trevor's daydream.

Trevor gritted his teeth. After all, they couldn't stand here forever posturing, but he sure didn't want the moment to end. He knew she was aroused, but it would stand to reason she would be feeling awkward about her body's reaction to the two of them. The irony of the situation was not lost on Trevor. He'd shared many women with Justin, and never had they had to tread so lightly before. Usually when they got home with a lady, they got right to business. The women they'd dated had known what the cards held. Hell, they'd asked for it. Now here they were with the one female they would spend the rest of their lives with, and she wanted to go home. He almost chuckled. Almost. They had no choice but to bide their time with her. Ease her into their lifestyle. Trevor just prayed that "ease" was relatively short term.

"I mean, I have to get up early, and it's getting late." She glanced at both men.

"On a Sunday? Do you have classes or something that meet on Sundays?" As much as Trevor hated the idea of ever having her out of his sight again, he forced himself to retreat a scant few inches.

"No. I have a mock meet tomorrow morning. Justin's coming to watch. You could come along also... If you want." Kara bit her lip. So hard it turned white.

Oh, we're so going to get along just fine, the three of us. Just as soon as we break the news to her...

66

"Sounds interesting. I just might." No need to sound overeager.

~

Kara stared at first Justin and then Trevor. There was an energy in the air. These guys were so close to each other it seemed as though they could read each other's minds. They reminded her of twins. Some people believed twins could communicate silently with each other.

As though they had discussed the matter thoroughly and come to some sort of decision, they both pronounced "okay" at the same moment.

Kara didn't know whether to be relieved or disappointed at their easy acquiescence to her departure.

"I'll drive you back to your car."

Kara turned her head to face Justin. "Thank you."

No one moved.

Three mouths hung slightly open. Three sets of eyes scanned back and forth between one another. Three distinct levels of breathing filled the silent space, each heavily panting as though they had just engaged in a threesome and were now attempting recovery.

The emotions Kara felt were intense and she needed to break the spell before she made a fool of herself. Ducking from beneath Justin's possessive arm, Kara made her way toward the exit. She called over her shoulder, "Coming?"

Neither man spoke, but she sensed they were on her heels without turning around. Facing them was too risky at the moment. Clearly she had lost her marbles.

As she rounded the house and approached the truck, only one set of steps continued to follow her. Justin's aftershave lingered in the air, his own outdoorsy scent mixing with expensive cologne.

Kara turned finally when she heard Trevor address her from a few steps back, angling toward the house. "Nice to meet you."

"Yes, you too." *More than you'll ever know.*

How could she ever see either of these men again? She couldn't believe her traitorous body was actually creaming over two hunks.

Kara reached for the door handle as she arrived at the side of the black truck gleaming in the moonlight, but Justin was quick to lay his hand on top of hers and pull the lever for her. His heat immediately reignited the flames that had only barely begun to simmer during the short walk to the front of the house. "Let me get that for you."

"Where did you learn such manners? Your mother must have had *some* influence over you." Even Kara's father was not as polite.

Justin's deep rumbling chuckle resonated a few inches from her ear as he helped her into the pickup and reached across her to buckle her in. "She did actually. She insisted all her kids have manners. If we didn't toe the line, we had to repeat the task until we got it right. You should have seen us leaving the kitchen table and returning over and over again until we could manage to keep our elbows off and chew with our mouths shut."

Before pulling away, he paused to press his lips once more against her mouth. It started as a gentle peck, but as soon as his mouth landed against Kara's she tilted her head to one side. Unable to stop herself, she actually moaned.

With both hands, she grasped Justin's arms and deepened the kiss, opening her mouth to let her tongue swipe over his full lips. The result was not disappointing. Justin pressed firmer against her and dipped his tongue into every crevice of her mouth, devouring her like a starving man. He grasped her shoulders in a firm grip, as though preventing her escape…or perhaps keeping himself from wandering to other parts of her body. She found she desperately wanted him to, but he was being such a gentleman.

Abruptly Justin stopped and pulled back, breathing heavily.

"Wow," he muttered, staring intently into Kara's eyes.

Kara's heart was going to pound out of her body. She'd never slept with a man on the first date before, or the second for that matter, but she sure wanted to get naked with this man right now. Unfortunately, she was acutely aware she also wouldn't mind getting naked with his roommate. The thought made her shiver in her seat. How was she ever going to face Justin if she also had such strong feelings for Trevor? This was not going to work. Besides, she would be graduating in a week and had no idea where she would go from there. She had applied for teaching positions at several schools near her parents' house in Portland as well as here in Corvallis, but hadn't heard back from anyone yet.

After staring at her for numerous moments, Justin finally pulled away, shut her car door, and headed for his side. She actually felt guilty, as though he could have read her mind trailing to naughty thoughts of his roommate.

In the silence, Kara shivered and glanced out the window into the night. Once again, she had the strangest feeling someone was watching her. The same intense fleeting sensation she'd had last night in the parking lot of Boot Scooters. And just like that it was gone.

Justin climbed into his side of the truck and peered out the front windshield before turning to look out the rear also. His brow was furrowed and his grip on the steering wheel tensed. Did he also get the feeling someone was spying on them?

Finally, he turned his gaze to her once again and smiled. "I had a really nice time. I hope you did, too."

"Definitely. And now I can say I've actually touched a cow." *That's so very sexy, Kara.*

Justin just laughed, a full hearty laugh that rumbled in his chest as he leaned his head back. The deep musical quality of his voice was like a soothing balm to her soul. It felt wonderful.

"Now there's something to tell your friends about," he joked as he started the engine. Within moments, they were backing out of the yard.

Barry stood in the shadows of the night. Far enough away he could not hear their words. He didn't want to attract any unnecessary attention. Hopefully his own smell would be masked by the numerous animals between himself and the three unsuspecting stars of his current nightmare. He watched Justin drive away with the hot blonde from last night and seethed with anger.

At thirty-five, Barry had now spent nearly two thirds of his life on a mission to avenge his parents' death. Never had he taken much time for himself. Never had he spent more than one night with a woman to warm his bed. He finally found a woman worth having for himself, and the objects of his life's mission thought to have her for themselves? Never. He had to put a stop to this. His revenge would be even sweeter now. First he would take her for his own. Then he would kill Trevor and Justin. Perhaps a slow death. Maybe tie them up and cut some important vein and make them watch as they slowly died while he fucked the woman of their current wet dreams right in front of them.

Patience. He needed to wait for just the right time. And, he needed help.

～

Justin looked over his shoulder. Was it possible someone was watching him? Following him? Or Kara? The same distinct smell of another wolf, one he was definitely unfamiliar with, hung in the air. Why did he feel so suspicious? It was quite likely one of his employees had a friend or lover from another pack.

Next to him was the woman he was going to spend his life worshipping. He and Trevor. He couldn't resist turning his thoughts back to her and her heat in his truck.

Thank God she was clearly aroused by both of them. He didn't know what he would've done if the feeling hadn't been mutual. Of course it would have been inconceivable, but still, he breathed a sigh of relief the bond was obviously felt by all three parties. Sure, it was against her nature, but she would not be able to avoid the draw. They would quickly squelch her trepidation concerning what her body was insisting was "right." As soon as the three of them consummated the mating.

Lord, she smells fantastic. The combination of her perfume and her arousal was keeping Justin's dick as hard as it had ever been in his life. A permanent state of arousal he was going to have to remedy by himself when he got back home.

Judging by his nose, her panties were soaked. Justin couldn't wait to get a taste of her. Run his tongue along her wet slit and lap up all the come flowing out of her horny body.

Justin reached for Kara's hand and held it while he drove. Every time he touched her, he could feel the growing connection between them. Their bodies were already beginning the bonding process. Making love for the first time would finalize it. For all three of them. The difficult part would be convincing this sweet mate of theirs that they needed to take her at the same time, filling both her pussy and her sexy ass to finalize the mating.

He shook thoughts of being inside her to the side and broke the comfortable silence. "I can't wait to see you in action tomorrow." *And I'm not talking about gymnastics.*

"I hope you aren't too disappointed. I'm not like the queen of gymnastics or anything. You'll see some really good gymnasts."

Justin glanced over to see her staring at him, her teeth nibbling again on her lower lip. He had to grit his teeth to withstand the need to pull the car over and suck her lower lip into his mouth. He wouldn't, because he knew he could not stop there.

"I'm sure you're fantastic. Besides, I won't notice the other gymnasts, so how will I be able to compare?" He chuckled as though the statement were a sappy line, but in reality, he was not kidding.

"Ha ha…" She fidgeted, her fine ass wiggling against the seat. "Your roommate seems nice. Do you think he'll really come with you tomorrow?"

"I'm sure he will." *Wild horses couldn't keep him away.*

Kara squeezed his hand tighter, tensing her entire body. She turned to look out the window, hiding her expression.

All too soon, Justin pulled into the parking lot where Kara indicated she'd left her car. He jumped out, rounded the truck to let her out before she could unbuckle, and then walked her across the gravel, his hand on her lower back.

Justin had maintained some sort of contact with Kara

almost from the moment she entered the restaurant earlier and he wasn't looking forward to releasing her now.

"Thanks for dinner." Kara turned her face up to his, and he leaned against the door to prolong the moment.

"You're very welcome. Next time I'll cook for you." Justin moved his hands up to cup her cheeks and bring her face closer to his.

"You cook, too?"

"Of course. Did you see someone hanging around the house who looked like a personal chef?" He smiled at her.

She didn't comment, but boldly leaned in to initiate the next kiss herself.

What started out hesitant quickly turned into a heated merging of tongues and warm lips. When Justin sucked gently on Kara's tongue, she moaned and leaned into his body against the car.

Justin spread his legs to accommodate her between them and dragged his hands down to her back and then lower to settle just above her tight ass. He wanted to do more, wanted to reach under her dress and touch her arousal, but he held himself firmly in check. *Tomorrow.* There was no way in hell he would be able to hold himself one more day past tomorrow. As it was she could not possibly be unaware of his rock-hard erection pressing into her firm stomach.

Kara finally broke off the kiss. Justin couldn't have done it if he'd wanted to. "Hmm. You're a fantastic kisser. I can hardly bring myself to get into my car and drive away."

Justin groaned. Lord, she was making this difficult for him. "Hon, don't say things like that. I'm trying to be a gentleman here. You need your sleep. I'll see you tomorrow." The words ached coming from his lips. Had he ever in his life turned down a woman who'd wanted him? Not that he could recall.

"Okay." Kara pulled back.

When Justin released her, his chest actually hurt at the lost contact. He forced himself to open her door and let her get inside.

Kara merely smiled up at him and muttered, "Tomorrow then."

Justin stood rooted to the spot as she drove away.

CHAPTER 6

"Holy mother of God." Trevor peered through the space between two fingers as he held his hand in front of his eyes. "What the hell was that?"

Justin sat beside Trevor, but didn't answer. A glance in his direction revealed he too was stunned, frozen in his seat, gritting his teeth, gripping the back of the chair in front of him.

Well, at least I'm not the only one who has an issue with this...this...kamikaze shit.

"That was a front handspring, round off, full twisting layout." Trevor lowered his hand and turned to the blonde middle-aged woman seated in front of him at the same time as Justin.

"Sorry. I overheard you. You must be new to the sport?" She smiled and nodded in their direction. "Yeah. I can tell by the looks on your faces you are. I'm Leila. Leila Anderson. My daughter is the one on the beam over there." She pointed to the right. Then she looked back at Trevor and chuckled. "Don't worry. You'll get used to it."

Trevor could only shake his head. "I don't think so."

Leila looked like she had probably been a gymnast herself, about twenty years ago. She simply laughed again.

Trevor watched in stunned silence while his mate, the woman he would spend the rest of his life with, or hers if she weren't careful, performed one death-defying feat after another.

"Dude, she's a professional. She's been doing this her entire life. I'm sure she's fine. I'm sure she knows what she's doing." Justin's words might have sounded convincing, to a member of some other species, but not to Trevor. He could hear the underlying fear in Justin's voice. The man was not one iota more comfortable with this than he was.

Perky blonde Leila laughed again and turned back to them. "Kara? She knows exactly what she's doing. She's such a sweet girl. Is she dating one of you?"

"Yes." Trevor didn't give her any additional information and the confused look on Leila's face spoke volumes, but he didn't offer any more details.

Kara moved from warming up on the floor to warming up on the bars. The momentary relief Trevor experienced knowing she would no longer be diving headfirst into the floor was quickly extinguished when she flung herself around first one bar and then another higher bar.

"Seriously, dude. I can't watch this. How many more days did she say she was going to participate in this shit?" Trevor decided it would be best to keep his conversation with Justin silent to avoid any more misunderstandings with Leila.

"One more week." Justin didn't look in Trevor's direction. He couldn't move his gaze from Kara's position on that damn high bar. Trevor lowered his own gaze to the floor for about sixty seconds, until his buddy finally

released his breath, assuring Trevor the imminent danger had passed.

Sure enough, Kara stood to the side now, waiting on another crazy teammate to perform Evel Knievel-like stunts. When the next girl landed on her butt under the bars, Trevor winced.

After Kara took her turn on the vault, flipping through the air, twisting and turning so many times the naked eye couldn't count them, and then the beam, where she clearly had a pact with the devil concerning her head and neck, Trevor nearly came out of his seat.

There was a pause before the actual "meet" would begin and Kara wandered over to greet them.

"Hi. You came. Both of you." She looked flushed and embarrassed. Shy.

"Of course," Justin piped up. "I told you I would. I even managed to drag my conflicted roommate along."

"Conflicted? What's he conflicted about?" Kara looked at Trevor with a confused face.

"Nothing. Don't worry about it." *"Shut the fuck up, you asshole,"* He added for Justin's "ears" only. *"The only thing I'm conflicted about is whether I want to be on top first or on bottom."*

Shit, she was so hot. Trevor had only seen her one time. Last night. And she'd had more clothes on than she did right now. His balls ached as she leaned closer. She smelled fantastic. Even sweaty she had her own unique scent that would drive Trevor crazy for the rest of his life. Her leotard thingy was...tight.

Didn't she own anything less...revealing?

On the other hand, the view was magnificent, and there were no other men around who were going to get anywhere near her again in this lifetime, so what did it matter?

"Did you enjoy the warm-ups? I wasn't at my best, but you should see a pretty good meet." Kara stepped back. Her eyes darted between Justin and Trevor. "It will only take about an hour. There aren't very many of us here today."

"I don't know anything about gymnastics, but from here I thought you looked great." Justin sounded tense, even to Trevor. Hopefully Kara wouldn't notice. The last thing they needed was for her to mess up and land on her head because her "beaux" were stressed out in the stands.

"Okay, well I have to get back with the team. I'll see you afterward?"

"Of course. We'll be right here."

An hour and a half later, Justin waited with Trevor by the door to the women's locker room. His head pounded from the stress of watching their lifemate's suicidal mission. He stretched his neck back and forth to release some of the strain. It didn't work.

Finally Kara came out the door. Beaming. "What did you think?" She directed the question at Justin first and glanced in Trevor's direction next. The lines above her eyebrow spoke volumes.

"It was… Well, I was… Hmm…scary?" Justin hoped the words wouldn't sound insulting. He held his breath and locked his gaze on his mate. Her hair was damp from a recent shower and the scent of her floral shampoo made Justin lean toward her. She wore a sexy skirt and top, showing off her very perfect figure. Justin ached to run his hands under her skirt.

Kara laughed. "That's an interesting response. The first of its kind I believe. Were you frightened? Of my gymnastics?"

"I...um...yes." Justin felt incredibly articulate at the moment.

"Sorry." Kara chuckled. "I don't mean to make light of your...affliction. I guess I should be pleased you... um...care."

"Well, I do, and—"

"Watch it, buddy. Don't say too much." Trevor silently interrupted the speech Justin was about to give Kara.

"And what?" Kara inquired.

"And... Do you want to come over for a late lunch? I promise not to serve any cows you've met." Justin released a breath and paused on the exhale to study Kara's face.

Would she accept? Or make things difficult for them? Either way, time was running out for Justin, and surely for Trevor. There was no way they could hold off having her for much longer. It would be simpler to lead her into their lifestyle gently, but slow was not in his current vocabulary.

"I'd love to."

"Thank God." Trevor's thoughts of relief mirrored Justin's.

Kara lifted her gym bag over her right shoulder. Justin reached to take it from her and, with a wave of his hand, gestured her to follow Trevor's lead.

"Should I take my own car? That way you two...I mean you," she glanced back at Justin behind her, cheeks reddened, "won't have to drive back to campus later."

"No. No. It will be fine. I don't mind taking you home." *It just won't be tonight...* Hopefully, if things went as he expected, after tonight her life would be forever changed.

From his hiding spot across the crowded parking lot, Barry watched Justin and Trevor walk out the door with Kara.

Oh yeah, he knew her name now. He'd done his research. Too bad he couldn't have watched her from the stands today. He'd bet she was sexier than ever in a leotard. But he couldn't take the chance Justin or Trevor would notice him.

As it was, they were suspicious. He knew they could smell his scent everywhere they went. They looked around, their hackles up. Let them shake in their boots a little. Made the game that much more fun.

He'd never been this close to them. Had always followed their lives from afar. Originally, he'd wanted to kill Trevor immediately. Slit his throat and be done with the little thug. But he knew knocking out one five-year-old orphan would not be nearly as sweet as waiting until the bastard was old enough to understand. Old enough to learn the truth about his own parents. Old enough to make it worthwhile to take the asshole's life in revenge for all the pain and suffering brought on by the actions of his parents.

Over the years the prize had gotten even better. Barry fully intended to go after Justin too, just to piss Trevor off. Give him a dose of what it was like to lose someone you care about. Now the ante was getting better by the day. After these two mated with the hot little blonde, it would be pure torture to take *her* away from Trevor also. Barry had big plans.

Shaking himself from his pondering, Barry looked through the binoculars once again, keeping an eye on his subjects.

She was leaving with them. Those unsuspecting bastards intended to bond with her, and soon. No matter, the bond would be broken after he killed them anyway. Then he could take the prize, spoils of war if you wish, and start his life anew.

Both men glanced around the parking lot before entering the truck. Did they sense him? He had masked his scent to the best of his abilities. Nevertheless, the two looked suspicious. Their noses were in the air. Good. Let them sweat. This was going to be fun.

CHAPTER 7

Kara rode between Justin and Trevor in the front of Justin's truck. The same truck he used last night to show her the dairy farm for the first time. Only this time, she was acutely aware of not one, but two sexy men, both currently touching her thighs. Neither seemed remotely chagrined by the idea.

Luckily the sound of country music coming from the speakers, coupled with the bumpy ride toward the farm, lessened the silence and eliminated the need for constant conversation to fill the lull.

Kara had dressed in a rather short, lightweight summer skirt and a white tight-fitting, V-necked T-shirt. She had been warm at the time, but now she was...so much warmer. Had her outfit been a good idea? Sitting between the two hunks, Kara held her hands in her lap and stared down at the amount of thigh sticking out. The friction against the jeans rasping her skin on both sides was sending goose bumps down her legs and making her wet with need.

She leaned her head back against the seat and closed

her eyes. What the hell was the matter with her? Never in her life had she pondered the idea of a ménage. Why now? How could not one, but two, men make her so incredibly aroused? More aware of her body's response than ever before?

What was she going to do with herself? She no longer felt a singular attraction for Justin. There was no way she could deny she wanted Trevor just as badly. What kind of a slut was she?

"Are you tired?" Justin broke the silence and laid a hand on her exposed leg to squeeze her muscle. The contact was so intimate fireworks shot off inside Kara. Moisture pooled in a desert, so dry for such a long time. The number of oases she had stumbled upon in the last few days was mindboggling. No man had ever elicited such a response from her before. And here she sat with two men, either of which could single-handedly have caused a waterfall to run freely down her legs. And had.

"Not really. Just…relaxed, I guess." *Would they buy that?*

"We're almost there. Then you can relax all you want while we cook you a nice meal. You must be starving after all those…acrobatics."

Kara laughed at their naiveté. "Tumbling."

Justin glanced at her and gave her a warm smile, melting her insides just a little bit more, if possible.

His hand, still resting on her thigh, stroked her skin. Kara stiffened and held her breath, afraid she would start moaning at any second. His thumb moved in a circular pattern on her leg and made her feel like her heart would beat clear out of her chest. And his pinky…the tiny little digit seared a path between her legs mere inches from her burning hot core.

Kara warred with herself. Part of her wanted to slip down farther in the seat and press her now-drenched panties against his hand. The other, more reasonable part screamed she was sitting next to his best friend, and for Christ's sake, lusting after him also.

By the time Justin pulled into the gravel area to the side of the house, Kara was nearly panting. She didn't actually believe her legs were going to hold her up when they got out of the car.

~

Justin pulled the truck, as quickly as possible, to the side of the house, biting the inside of his cheek to keep from coming in his pants. His hard on was rigid enough to rival any hard on in the history of mankind.

"*Holy mother, she-s so fucking hot. I can smell her essence leaking out of her. She's drenched. Practically moaning.*" Trevor shifted in the seat, probably trying to adjust his own hardening dick on Kara's right side.

"*Yeah. Let's just hope she doesn't freak out when she finds out who and what we are...and what we expect from her.*" Justin parked and grabbed for the door handle. Perhaps a little outside air would soothe his burning skin. *Not.*

He jumped down from the truck lightning fast, as if there were a poisonous snake in the cab. With a deep breath, he turned to take Kara's hand and help her down to the ground while Trevor made a similar hasty exit from the other side.

The cool breeze outside was a relief from the tension-filled cab of the truck.

"Shall we?" Justin pulled Kara's hand and headed toward the house. "You must be hungry." *I know I am.* It was almost one p.m. and he was fairly starving. Though for the life of him Justin was not sure what he would prefer to eat first, hamburgers or Kara's hot wet pussy.

What would she do if he set her up on the counter and spread her legs for his feasting? What would she do if Trevor sucked her ripe nipples at the same time?

A shiver went down Justin's spine all the way to his toes. *"Man, this is going to be a long fucking afternoon of wooing."*

"You ain't kidding," was Trevor's only response.

CHAPTER 8

After lunch, Kara found herself lounging on the patio behind the house. She couldn't believe how her body was responding to these men, in their house. She had gone outside to escape the incredible pull she had to both of them. A respite from the constant attentions of two of the sexiest guys on the planet. Her confusion over her feelings toward them was mounting and making her nervous. And why did neither of them seem fazed by the other? She would've thought by now Justin would've sucker punched his friend for flirting with her mercilessly.

Throughout lunch, each man had taken turns catering to her every need, ensuring she was never out of anything, that she was comfortable. She'd felt like a princess. *It's too bad I can't have both of them.* Kara chuckled to herself. The impossible thought sent liquid heat through her bloodstream. She closed her eyes and wondered what it would be like to have both of them catering to her *sexual* needs, at the same time. *Oh God. Where the hell did that come from?* Kara was a one-man woman. Wasn't she?

"Kara?" Justin approached her and she had to squint into the afternoon sun to see his face. "Are you okay?"

"Yes. I'm fine. Just…exhausted," she lied. What was she supposed to tell him? *Well, Justin, I'm struggling with wanting both you and your roommate to strip me naked right here and have your way with me.* Surely Justin would run off.

Justin leaned down and gently pushed Kara forward to make room to straddle the soft cushions of the lounge chair and nestle himself behind her. He pulled her back against his chest, and she couldn't help a sigh from escaping her lips. He was so warm and comfortable. She felt calm. At peace. Home. Except for the fact her mind kept wandering to Trevor. Where was he?

Justin's hands skimmed up and down Kara's arms, so gently she could barely feel them. Just enough pressure to make her shiver. The hair on her arms stood on end. He leaned in to nibble her neck and she found herself tilting her head to one side to give him better access. *Hmmm…* It felt so good. So…right.

Kara twisted slightly in front of Justin to bring her lips to his. She needed his mouth on hers. Needed to taste him. Like her life depended on it.

As soon as their lips came together, the desire intensified. Like a starving woman, Kara moaned around the kiss and pressed herself into Justin's body. She was completely at the mercy of…she had no idea what. But she couldn't stop this madness, even if she wanted to. Her heavy eyes drifted closed.

Justin's hand cupped Kara's face and held her chin gently but firmly. The kiss intensified. His tongue lightly brushed the edge of her lips and she found herself opening to him. Allowing him to enter her greedy mouth. God, she wanted him. She'd never wanted anything in her life as much as she wanted this.

She stretched her legs out in front of her on the lounge chair, but the heat between them was scorching her.

When Justin finally broke the kiss, it was to let his mouth wander down her chin and over to her ear. His warm breath streamed rhythmically into and around the lobe. A shiver ran through her entire body.

When Justin's hands moved down Kara's arms and onto her thighs, she thought she would combust. She even pulled her legs slightly apart to allow him access to her center, like a wanton woman. A soft moan escaped her lips. It surprised her.

Sensing movement, Kara's eyes opened slowly to find Trevor wandering in their direction. His shirt was off, his glorious bronze chest exposed to her perusal. She sucked in a breath at the thought of the scene he was walking onto.

Unable to stop herself, her gaze meandered down Trevor's body. His jeans were unbuttoned and hanging low on his hips. So sexy. He had no shoes or socks on. When she allowed her gaze to return upward, she found herself staring at his expression. *Lust.* He wanted her. How was this possible? Was she dreaming?

Justin wrapped his arms around Kara's middle just under her breasts. She could feel their heaviness against his forearms and ached to have him grasp them in his hands. Her shirt felt several sizes too small, and her lace bra abraded her nipples and sent a shiver down her spine.

He placed his chin on her shoulder, and Kara turned her face to see he was looking at Trevor, just as she had been. With lust in his gaze. *Huh?* Shouldn't he be telling Trevor to take a hike?

Kara's gaze returned to follow Trevor as he sat sideways on the end of her chair. Instinctively she pulled her legs back into an Indian-style position to make room for him. Trevor leaned to his side on one hand, brushing against Kara's exposed leg. Sparks shot up her thighs and ignited in her womb.

She held very still, breathing shallow breaths, waiting for whatever these hunks were going to say. She wasn't sure whether she wanted them to say this wasn't going to work out because they both wanted her...or that it *was*.

No one spoke for several moments. Kara could feel her heart pounding in her chest. All three of them were breathing like they had just run a mile.

"Kara..." Justin began, "...we...Trevor and I..." He cleared his throat. "What I'm trying to say is that...you might have noticed we're both very much attracted to you."

Kara nodded against Justin's chest below his chin. She stared into Trevor's eyes.

Trevor cautiously reached one hand out and laid it on Kara's thigh. "We think the feeling is mutual, babe." He raised one eyebrow in question. His blond hair fell across his forehead in the breeze and his dark green eyes bore into hers, waiting.

"I..." Liquid heat leaked between her legs. *Yes.* She gripped Justin's biceps with her hands.

"It's okay," Justin whispered into Kara's ear, eliciting a shiver that spread through her entire body. "Let us take care of you." He nibbled her ear and loosened his hold on her middle to spread his hands across her abdomen, his thumbs brushing the undersides of her needy breasts.

Kara gasped. *What is happening to me?* She felt like a slut. A pampered, wanton, needy slut.

Trevor inched slowly closer and lightly placed both hands on Kara's folded shins. "I can smell your arousal, babe. I want to taste you."

Heat burned through Kara's chest and face. Was she really going to let these two men ravish her? Those piercing green eyes staring at her were feral. At that moment Trevor reminded her of a large dog. She could almost see his tongue hanging out ready to lap at her.

She was powerless to stop the madness. *You know you want this. Let it go.*

Justin reached his large rough hands under Kara's tight shirt and spread them once again over her stomach, this time against her bare skin.

Meanwhile, Trevor separated Kara's tangled ankles and pushed them apart to straddle the seat. He moved into the V of her legs and let his hands run up her thighs.

"I..." She just couldn't form any words. What the hell was she supposed to say? *Don't? Don't stop?*

Justin's lips ran a trail from her ear down to her neck. Kara let her eyes fall shut and leaned against his chest. His thumbs slowly crawled their way under her bra to rub against her sensitive skin. "I know, hon. Relax."

Large hands suddenly covered her sensitive breasts and squeezed.

At the same time, Kara felt warm breath on her legs moments before lips nibbled a path up her inner thigh. God *almighty*. Kara thought she would explode. And her clothes were still on. Sensations bombarded her.

"Raise your arms, hon," Justin mumbled in her ear. She was powerless to do anything but obey as he pulled her shirt over her head. A slight breeze cooled her burning skin.

When she opened her eyes, the sight in front of her was so erotic it made her gasp. Her skirt bunched up at her waist. Trevor was licking a path up her thigh, and her chest heaved, causing her erect nipples to bounce up and down under the thin lace of her pink bra.

Justin's thumb brushed her lower lip and slipped into her open mouth. She couldn't keep from sucking the digit into her warmth. For the first time in her life, she found herself actually *wanting* to suck on a man's cock. Justin's. Or Trevor's. Or both.

"Mmmm." The noise filling the air was her moan of desire.

"Oh, God, baby. That's so hot." Trevor lifted his face to hers without raising himself from his spot between her legs. "I want you so bad. I have to taste you." His fingers trailed up Kara's thighs, gripped her pink lace thong, and gave a quick yank to remove the material.

"Oh, my God." Trevor growled. "Her pussy is bare. And…she's glistening with her juices."

"Fuck." Justin leaned down to see Kara's mons while she shivered under their gazes.

How can this be so incredibly erotic?

"I…shave…"

"I see that, love." Trevor blew a breath over her exposed sex, and Kara lifted her hips toward his mouth, begging him to touch her.

"For gymnastics…"

"That's so hot," Justin started, "I want to watch you, Trev. Take her skirt off."

Kara found herself quickly lifted a few inches in Justin's big arms while Trevor pulled her legs back onto the chair and then removed her skirt. In less than a heartbeat, he had her spread out before him once again, her legs straddling the lounger. Her sex open wide to his inspection.

A quick snap opened the front clasp of Kara's bra and Justin tossed the lingerie to the side. He pinned her arms beneath his own and reached forward to pinch her nipples.

"Oh…God…" Kara lolled her head back and moaned.

"Watch me, baby. Watch me suck your sweet little clit into my mouth." Trevor was staring into her face when she opened her eyes to look down at him. A film seemed to separate them. The language he was using was not something she was accustomed to, but it ratcheted her arousal higher to hear him speak so candidly.

Trevor ran one finger through the glistening wetness pouring from her opening and she nearly shot off the chair.

Firm hands grasped her breasts and pinched her nipples. Another set of fingers grasped her thighs, pushed her open as wide as they could, and held her in place.

"Eyes on me," Trevor repeated. The command made Kara's blood boil with need. She had never thought of herself as submissive before, but the scene unfolding was the most erotic event of her life. Sure, she'd had several floundering experiences with men, or more like boys, experimenting with sex in high school and early college. She wasn't a prude. She just hadn't found anyone who really rocked her world the way she would have liked. And for more than a year, she'd been too busy finishing up school and concentrating on gymnastics to care. However, nothing in her past could have compared to what was happening here.

Finally, after a painstakingly slow examination of Kara's exposure, Trevor ran his tongue over her aching clitoris, keeping a firm grasp on her legs to keep her from struggling against him. Using his forearms to steady her movement, he reached with his long fingers to spread her open and then dipped his tongue inside her.

Kara thought she would surely die. "I need...please..."

"You need what, hon? Tell us what you need." Justin whispered the words into her ear and twisted her burning nipples between his thumbs and forefingers.

"I... Oh, God...please..."

Trevor chuckled. "We're going to have to teach her to be more specific in the future."

Kara glared at Trevor. *Please don't make me say more.*

"Don't worry. I'll take pity on you this time." He smiled at her while pushing one long finger into her core and then twisting it before dragging it back out. "Like that? Is that what you want?"

"Uhh…" Kara strained to raise her hips.

So many sensations assaulted her all at once, she couldn't concentrate on any one thing. Justin kneaded and pinched her breasts and nipples to the point of pain. The pain felt fantastic though. She craved more.

Trevor stuck two fingers inside Kara's soaking center and then leaned down to suck her throbbing clit hard into his mouth.

The action made Kara scream and buck as the orgasm washed over her, Trevor's unrelenting tongue flicking repeatedly over her engorged nub. As she rode out the waves of the longest and best orgasm of her life, Trevor continued to flick her clit and drag his fingers over the most sensitive spot inside her.

As she finally came down from the natural high, sweat ran down her face, in spite of the cool afternoon air. Justin brushed sticky hair back from her cheeks and whispered into her ear. "God, that was so hot, hon. I need you so bad."

The evidence of his "need" was poking Kara in the back, and she longed to have him buried deep inside her. The recent orgasm only fueled her need. Kara twisted to look into his deep chocolate eyes. "I want to taste you." The bold words escaped her lips before she could think, and she bit her bottom lip at the admission.

"And you shall." Justin leaned around to kiss her, a steamy kiss that skipped right over gentle and quickly became urgent. Heated. His tongue drove into her mouth and searched every corner. He groaned against her and then pulled away almost as fast as he had pressed into her.

"Hold her for me, would you?" Justin directed the question at Trevor and when Kara turned toward him, she found Trevor had somehow already managed to strip his jeans off and was now kneeling forward reaching for her. His bronzed skin was glorious. Every inch of him was tan. Or was that his natural color? He didn't even have tan lines. Did he lie out in the nude? The thought brought new heat to her core.

"I want some of that." Trevor leaned in and took Kara's mouth in another kiss, her lips still wet from Justin's ravishing. Trevor's mouth was only slightly gentler. His tongue circled the opening, and she could taste her salty essence on his lips. Somehow the idea was incredibly sexy. He gripped her biceps gently to hold her forward while Justin climbed out from behind her.

Moments later, Justin situated himself behind Kara once again, his hard, tight chest pressed to her back.

Justin reached around Kara, skimmed his hands down her body, and dipped one finger from each hand inside her. While her gaze followed his hands, he brought them back up to his mouth and sucked them clean. "Mmm. You taste delicious."

"I can attest to that," Trevor confirmed. "Now flip over, babe." Trevor tugged on Kara who held a look of shock on her face.

Justin loved how she was so pure. She'd never had any experience remotely like this one. She may have had sex before, but never had two men made love to her at the same time. And if her reaction to the mind-blowing orgasm was any indication, she hadn't had too many of those either.

"Hon, we want to make you feel good. Face me. I want to watch your sexy breasts in front of you while Trevor presses into you from behind."

A brazen look of a far bolder woman took hold of Kara's face. "I think it's my turn, actually. You've both had your fun."

Kara flipped over between them, but immediately dipped her head to run her tongue from the base to the tip of Justin's enlarged cock.

"Oh, Christ, hon," Justin moaned. "You should really warn a guy before you do that." Kara paid no attention to him. She ran the tip of her tongue through the slit on the top of his aching shaft and then immediately lowered her mouth gently down the length of him. The feeling was exquisite torture. Justin had to grip the arms of the lounge chair to keep still. His balls drew up tight, threatening to send him into a full ejaculation from a single long suck into her fantastic mouth.

"Trevor, I'm not going to last. She is...fucking...incredible." Justin stared at his friend's face, communicating silently. Trevor did not take his eyes off Kara, however. He looked entranced by the beautiful Goddess on her knees leaning down to suck Justin off.

"Hang on. Let me get inside her tight pussy."

"Hang on? Are you kidding? There's no `hang on' here. Either get your dick in gear or you'll be late for this party."

Trevor smiled and reached for Kara's hips to lift them higher into the air.

Kara moaned around Justin's erection, driving him more insane. He reached out and grasped the back of her head to hold her steady for a moment.

"Hon, Trevor is going to enter you from behind while you suck my cock." Justin had to grit his teeth to avoid ejaculating into her mouth prematurely. Even without moving up and down, her tongue danced around the length of his erection, teasing him mercilessly. He grew unbelievably harder.

"Spread your legs farther apart, babe." Trevor nudged her thighs from the inside and reached between her legs to rekindle the passion of her barely concluded orgasm.

It must have worked because Kara raised her ass a little higher in the air in offering and sucked tightly, milking Justin harder.

"Now, Trevor. I'm going to blow."

Trevor reached for Kara's shoulder with one hand and used the other to angle his cock into her hot channel. In one thrust he was fully seated. "Shit. Baby, you're so tight."

Kara moaned desperately, the vibrations traveling Justin's length and forcing him to clench his teeth once more.

Justin watched as Trevor moved his hands to hold her hips steady and then groaned in pleasure as he pulled almost all the way out only to slam back inside her.

Justin squeezed his eyes shut and leaned his head against the seat cushion, desperately hanging on while Kara began an erotic rocking motion that repeatedly pushed her pussy over Trevor's dick and then her mouth over Justin's cock.

Justin wrapped the smooth curls of Kara's hair in his hands and struggled against applying too much pressure to her head. *Please don't stop.*

"Kara…baby…I can't…" Trevor let out a loud "ahhh" as his orgasm slammed into him.

At the same time, Justin reached between his body and Kara's, pinched her clit with two fingers and watched as her orgasm hit her full force. As soon as the waves of her climax slowed down, she sucked on Justin's cock like a starving woman.

He started to pull out of her mouth. "Baby, I'm gonna come."

She wouldn't let go. He had no expectations when it came to her swallowing him, but she was relentless. He reached his peak and allowed himself to ejaculate into her warm mouth. The view of Kara's lips surrounding his length while he grew slightly flaccid was the sexiest sight of his life. Finally, she collapsed on top of him, her arms and legs dangling off the sides of the lounger.

"God. That was…fantastic…" she managed to mumble against Justin's chest.

Justin chuckled. "You could say that."

"I'm not sure there's actually a word to describe what we just did." Trevor had sat back and was now running his hands over Kara's skin, teasing the backs of her thighs lightly.

"*Shit*." Kara lifted her head a few inches and looked around. "We're outside. Aren't there other people around? What if someone saw us?"

"It's Sunday, honey. No one's around right now. We may share with each other, but we don't share what is ours with others." Justin pulled Kara's face up toward his with soothing pressure on her jaw. Surely the look in his eyes would put a period on the end of that sentence for her.

She visibly swallowed. "Lord. I just had sex with your roommate in front of you." Pink filled her cheeks in embarrassment.

"Yes, and it was the hottest thing I've ever witnessed. And in a few minutes, I'm going to have my turn sliding into your tight pussy while Trevor fondles you."

Kara gulped. "Isn't this a little…weird?"

"Weird is only what people make it. Did this feel weird to you?" Justin silently begged her to say "no."

"Well…no, but… I mean, I've heard of threesomes of

97

course, but this is more, more..." She pushed herself to a sitting position and crossed her arms over her chest. Now that they weren't in the heat of passion, she'd grown modest.

Trevor reached around Kara from behind and carefully grasped each wrist with his hands. He pulled them apart and up over her head. When he leaned forward to place his chin on her shoulder, he angled her arms behind his head to silently encourage her to grasp his neck. "Don't cover yourself with us, baby," he whispered in her ear, nibbling around her cheek and neck. "Your breasts are perfect," he continued as he reached around her to take one in each palm and weigh them with a little bounce.

Justin couldn't resist the urge to reach out and tweak the distended dainty pink nipples poking toward him. A light pinch sent a shiver through Kara's entire body, shaking all three of them.

"God, you're sexy. I love the innocence on your face when we do something unfamiliar to you. The shock." Justin would never get enough of her, even if they kept her tied to the bed for the rest of eternity.

"Let's move inside to a more comfortable spot." Trevor's tone indicated it wasn't a request. Although Justin knew neither he nor Trevor would ever do anything to hurt Kara or insult her independence, when it came to mating, there would always be a certain level of dominance the two men would command, brooking no argument.

It wouldn't matter because Kara would soon be completely theirs, though they had yet to explain the situation to her. Her body would never deny them anything. She would be powerless to fend them off for the rest of her life. She wouldn't want to, and the thought wouldn't occur to her. An impenetrable bond would connect her entire being to Justin and Trevor. As soon as they both penetrated her at the same time, she would be mated to them. Over the next few days the bond would increase as it grew stronger. As was the case with all matings, Kara was about to experience the most intense sexual urges of her life, and she didn't even know it yet...

As they stood with her, she seemed to falter and look around. A slight shudder ran through her body. The strange sensation seemed to pass just as quickly, Justin noted. Perhaps she was afraid someone was watching them. Why did he get the same feeling? Again?

"Do you smell someone, Trev? It's the fourth time I've smelled this particular wolf. Does one of our men, or women, have a new friend hanging around?" Justin hugged Kara's body close to his, suddenly feeling a bit self-conscious himself about their little display on the patio.

"Now that you mention it, I did catch the same whiff as we were leaving the gym earlier. I just assumed it could be anyone. But why would we notice it here? What are the chances?"

"Let's get Kara inside. One of us should check it out. Ask a few questions of the men." Justin lifted a sated Kara into his arms.

"You guys head in. I'll just grab our stuff and be right behind you." Trevor reached for their clothes as Justin backed away with Kara, but he didn't miss the concerned furrow between Trevor's brows.

Oh, holy mother of God. Just watching Kara's sexy little body writhe beneath those two assholes made Barry's dick hard. As long as he ignored the men and focused solely on Kara, he was about to blow. And those idiots were so intent on taking her, they didn't notice the presence of another wolf in the area. Granted, he was very far away.

With all the cow dung between him and them, he was surprised they even glanced around after round one of coitus. And he knew more rounds were to come. Those assholes were undoubtedly about to seal the mating. He'd decided to wait it out. As much as he hated watching those two violating the woman he intended to have for himself, it would be that much sweeter taking her from them after the mating was complete.

Stick to the objective, Barry. Inflicting as much pain as possible on Trevor before his untimely demise.

What Barry needed now was assistance. No way in hell he could take on both Trevor and Justin alone. He needed help, someone who would be willing to go after them also.

CHAPTER 9

Kara felt like a princess. She was so sated she couldn't lift a muscle. And she didn't need to. Justin carried her cradled in his arms through the glass patio doors and down a long hall to what she assumed was the master bedroom.

The room was enormous and a huge mahogany bed, big enough to look proportional in the suite, dominated the center. The sheets were surely custom made because Kara had never seen anything so big before.

Justin gently lay her down in the center of the silky maroon comforter. It reminded her of a rose's deep red color.

"Be right back, hon." His voice was so seductive as she watched him disappear into what was surely the master bath. Kara relaxed back into the luxurious silk and sighed. *What the hell am I going to do now?*

Justin returned from the bathroom at the same time Trevor materialized from the hall. They both stretched out on the bed on either side of her, exchanging a long look between them and sending chills down her spine. *Whatever these two hunks have in mind is what I'm going to do now.*

Consequences be damned. She'd worry about the repercussions of this little ménage on her mental stability later.

Both men stroked her arms, barely touching her. Just enough to elicit goose bumps over her entire body. She could feel the burn in her sex rekindling. *How the hell is that possible so soon after two glorious orgasms?*

"Kara," Justin said, "there are things we need to tell you. Things you need to know..."

Kara stared into his brown eyes and saw the lust she could hear in his voice. He wanted her. He needed to be inside her. Now.

She reached for him, a magnetic pull driving her legs to widen and accept Justin into her core as she had Trevor. "It can wait. Whatever it is..."

A relieved breath escaped Justin's lips, and he leaned in to devour her mouth, a needy insistent kiss, almost rough, but not rough enough. The knot of fire in Kara's center made her buck her hips into the air, begging silently for either man to please touch her, again.

Another mouth joined Justin's on her face and then her lips as though Justin had passed the kiss off to his friend. Trevor's firm grip held her chin while he explored her tongue and lips in earnest.

Kara couldn't stand the intense physical response she had to these two. She needed to touch them, every part of them. She reached out to grab both men.

"Uh uh," Trevor muttered into Kara's mouth. Confusion clouded her mind until he grasped first one arm and then the other and planted them over her head. He held them tight with the hand he was leaning on, and resumed the lip seal he had created with her mouth.

Justin trailed kisses down Kara's stiff body as she lifted her ass off the bed. He gently pushed her hips back down with one commanding hand as he arrived at her aching breasts and sucked one tender nipple into his warm mouth. Firm pressure on her stomach kept Kara from bucking like a bronco beneath the onslaught of sensations. Trevor never ceased his hungry kisses, but his free hand reached down to fondle the second engorged mound reaching for attention. She wasn't large breasted, most gymnasts weren't, but the repeated stimulation was making her chest feel tight and swollen.

The two men were so in tune with each other. Clearly they had done this before. Why did that idea make her jealous? Without a word they alternately switched breasts so neither would be bereft of either the sucking or the fondling.

Kara squirmed uncontrollably, forcing Justin to shift himself between her legs. He blew warm air across one aching nipple and then reached with both hands to spread her thighs wider, sliding down her body until his face was inches from her needy center.

Kara squeezed her eyes shut and moaned against Trevor's mouth. "Please…" she muttered.

"Please what, honey?" Justin's breath was torturing her mons while his hands pressed her thighs wider and wider apart. He chuckled, a low rumble she could feel against her thighs. "Your pussy is the sexiest thing I've ever seen, shaved clean and glistening with your come. Did you know your fluids are running out onto the bed and I haven't even touched you yet? Do you know how hot it is for your sexy legs to be able to be spread so wide? I knew there was going to be some benefit to the ferocious tumbling I watched you do."

Kara groaned in frustration at his words. Words meant to enflame her and drive her further into a state of unbelievable *need*. And it was working. She arched, wiggling and squirming in vain against Justin's frustrating hold on her thighs.

Kara wretched her mouth to the side to separate from Trevor's roving tongue and demand relief. "Justin... please... Please suck my...clit...into your mouth. Please bite down on it... Please... I need you inside me. Put... something inside me..."

She lifted her gaze to Justin's and saw all the passion in his face her words incited. Wasn't this just some fantasy gone...perfect?

"Okay, honey." Justin dipped his head, sucked Kara's clit into his mouth and gently bit down on the little bundle, making her scream so loud the cows would surely hear.

Her third orgasm slammed through her, and as wave after wave of contractions gripped her inner walls, Justin quickly skimmed up her body and pushed himself inside her. It had been so long since she'd been with a man. She was so tight. And the feeling was wonderful... Arms still held firmly over her head, Kara's breasts jiggled against her chest. Trevor stroked them lightly while Justin held himself aloft and stared down into Kara's eyes with an expression of complete ownership. "Mine," he stated flatly. "Mine."

It seemed Kara could stare into Justin's soul through those deep chocolate eyes of his. She shivered at the growing connection she felt, not just with Justin, but with Trevor alongside her, as though all three were merging into one. She glanced over at Trevor, emerald eyes held her in a similar trance. Trevor's smile spread across his entire face. He seemed to know a secret she was about to be privy to. It was the warmest sensation, as if she were finally...home.

As Justin moved, Kara's body responded as though she hadn't just had three orgasms already. She jerked her gaze back to Justin as Trevor alternately pinched first one nipple and then the other, somehow sensing her need for more possessive contact.

A new level of intense sensation reached into her womb. Every movement inside her brushed against nerve endings not previously there. Kara heard an audible gasp come from deep inside her. She bucked beneath Justin, begging silently for relief. How was this possible?

An urgent thrusting began, sending Kara into another orgasm on the heels of the third. A sharp scream pealed through the air. It could only be hers. Kara gasped for breath to draw more oxygen into her lungs and slow her racing heart.

As her spasms wound down, Kara was able to concentrate once again on Justin's eyes. His face tensed moments later as he held his erection solidly inside her and pumped her full of his semen. The warm fluid seemed to continue to pour against her womb for an unbelievable length of time.

Thank God I'm on the pill. Nevertheless, she'd never had sex before without a condom. And here she'd had sex twice with two relative strangers. *How could I forget protection?*

Exhaustion was beginning to seep into Kara's system. When Justin gently pulled her into his embrace, she let him. When he lifted her to pull back the comforter, she let him. Both men settled down on either side of her. A busy day and four mind-blowing orgasms caught up with her, and she closed her eyes, promising herself a short nap would make the world seem much more focused later...

Justin stared down at Kara in wonder. How had he gotten

so lucky? He and Trevor could not have asked for circumstances to have turned out better than this.

Nudging his friend on the other side of Kara, Trevor made a motion with his head toward the door and the two gently slipped from between the sheets to stand. Kara made a soft slumberous sound, but simply snuggled farther under the covers. They'd been asleep for about an hour, but Justin was restless. His mind would not relax, knowing when she woke up they were going to have to confront the fact Trevor and Justin were not ordinary partners.

They needed a plan.

Both men reached to grab a pair of jeans, tugged them on, and slipped out the door to tread lightly down the hall and out of earshot.

"What do we do now, *stud*?" Trevor chuckled when they reached the kitchen.

"Ha, ha. I was hoping you had an idea. We have to tell her. It isn't right to keep up this 'normal' pretense for very long. She deserves to know the truth." Justin hoped his friend was on the same page. This was a serious issue.

"Perhaps we could just do a...sort of demonstration?" Trevor reached for the fridge handle and yanked the door open. He grabbed two bottles of water and tossed one to Justin.

"More importantly, I want to know why I keep sensing a wolf from another pack everywhere I go. I think I'll head over to the barn and see if anyone knows anything. It's starting to give me the creeps." Justin grabbed his boots by the door and sat at the table to pull them on.

A knock at the back screen door startled both men. Their foreman, Kyle, stood outside holding his cowboy hat in his hands.

Trevor motioned the man inside. "Kyle. What brings

you over? We don't usually see you on a Sunday afternoon."

"Actually, I just came by to check on one of the horses. She's about to foal."

"Ah, good. Is she all right?" Justin stared at the troubled look on Kyle's face, hoping the mare was okay.

"I haven't seen her yet. I found this taped to the barn door when I got here." Kyle held out a piece of paper.

Justin grabbed it and blinked in shock as he read the note. "'*Your days are numbered. Then the woman will be mine.*'"

Trevor snatched the paper and stared at it himself as if doubting Justin's ability to read. "What the hell?"

"Guess my gut was right." Fear gripped Justin's stomach and made it churn. "That's it? There was nothing else? Did you see anyone?"

"No." Kyle shook his head. "Whoever it was had already gone before I got there."

"Shit." Justin began to pace.

"Do you…" Kyle coughed, "…know who 'the woman' is?"

"That would be Kara—our mate."

"*Our* mate? As in both of you?"

"Yeah. Unusual, I know. But it seems we're a threesome." Justin's hands shook with anger. "I've been noticing another wolf in the area. I was about to head to the barn and see if anyone knew anything about it. Have you seen anyone suspicious? Do any of the men have a friend from another pack hanging around?"

Kyle's eyes widened. "No, not that I'm aware of. I haven't seen or heard anything."

"Why would anyone be threatening us?" Trevor looked at Justin.

"I have no idea, but we better call my parents and let them know what's going on. I haven't had a chance to talk to them since we met Kara. Though I'm sure Ryan gave them all the gory details from Friday night." Justin rolled his eyes.

"I don't think we should take any chances. I have a suspicion Kara is going to be none too happy when she finds out we'll be sticking to her like glue." Trevor's chuckle made Justin smile.

"Well, huh." Kyle reached for the door to leave, shaking his head in surprise. "I can't remember when one of our pack had two male wolf mates. Is she the human I smell in the air?"

"Yes," Trevor began, "she's sleeping in the other room."

"Congrats. I wish you all the best. I'll keep a sharp eye out around here."

"Thanks, man. We appreciate it." Justin walked Kyle out the back door and stood on the porch after Kyle entered the barn, staring into the trees. For the life of him, he couldn't imagine who would be interested in threatening them. But he aimed to find out.

Trevor leaned against the porch railing. "I think we should finish the bonding."

Justin nodded. "I agree. If there's a threat of any kind, we need to be sure we're solid. Being able to communicate with her remotely would make me feel a lot better."

Trevor pushed off the railing and headed inside. Justin followed at his back. He could hear water running as they cross the room. He smiled. "Looks like she's awake."

"I hope that's a bath running." Trevor pulled his shirt over his head and dropped it in the hall as he proceeded.

Justin imitated his roommate, his cock already stiffening at the thought of Kara naked in the bathroom, slipping into warm water.

~

Trevor wasted no time, stripping off his clothes as he moved down the hall, flinging them every which way until he reached the sound of running water. He paused in the doorway to the bathroom and sucked in a breath at the sight before him. His hands gripped the doorframe. Justin, just as naked as he was, halted behind him, and Trevor could hear heavy breathing as Justin peered over Trevor's shoulder to take in the view.

The sexiest creature alive was leaning over the huge whirlpool tub, testing the water. Her naked ass stuck out toward the men, begging to be fondled, begging to be *taken.*

Trevor advanced on Kara, Justin right beside him. There was no doubt the men had the same exact intent in mind. Kara flinched and turned quickly around to face them, her thick blonde curls bouncing around her angelic face.

Trevor spoke as he approached her, Justin flanking her on the other side. "Can we join you?"

Kara trembled. She licked her lips and then nodded. Arousal instantly flooded her pussy, the scent filling the bathroom.

Trevor fought the urge to moan. She had no idea what to do with the feelings suffocating her, but he knew she also couldn't deny him or Justin any more than they could ignore the need to bond with her. There was so much to be said, but it would change nothing. On some level Kara knew her life was about to change. Her trembling spoke volumes. Her eyes were wide and darted between them.

Justin reached out to take Kara into his arms. Trevor could see her quivering right in front of him. He might have been inclined to give her a few more days and not push the issue, if he hadn't also smelled her increasing arousal as soon as they entered the room. She wanted it just as badly as they did. Plus, finishing the mating would increase their ability to protect her.

"Relax." Justin tried to soothe her. "You know we would never hurt you. Let's get into the water. A nice soak will help you relax your muscles."

Justin stepped over the edge of the tub, pulling Kara with him. Trevor followed to Kara's back, sandwiching her between the two men.

As they sunk into the deep round Jacuzzi, Trevor ran his hands up and down her back, pausing at her neck to massage her stiff shoulders. He nearly came spontaneously when she moaned her pleasure and leaned her head against Justin's chest.

Trevor looked into Justin's eyes, a silent agreement passing between them. They knew exactly how they wanted to play this out. Trevor and Justin had shared women many times before. The idea was not new to them. But the intense feelings between them were. Never before had they had *this* woman and all she promised. Trevor shivered and felt his balls draw up tight against his body. He needed to prepare Kara for what was about to happen before he shot off in the water.

Smoothing his hands down Kara's back toward her ass, Trevor leaned in to whisper softly in her ear. "Just relax, baby. Let us take care of you."

"Mmmm," was her only response.

Trevor lifted Kara gently a few inches by the waist and let Justin adjust himself to sit on the bottom of the tub. He set Kara's small frame on Justin's lap, straddling him, her legs forced open, her thighs resting on Justin's, her ass open between Justin's knees. Warm water splashed around them, reaching the tips of Kara's nipples as she leaned into Justin's embrace. Trevor reached to turn the water off and pushed the button to start the jets. The soft whirr of pulsing water filled the room.

Justin grasped Kara's face to claim her mouth while Trevor let his fingers roam over her firm ass, circling closer and closer to the tight rear orifice on the verge of providing incredible pleasure for all three of them in a few short minutes.

Before touching her puckered virgin opening, Trevor let his hand reach under her farther and stroked his fingers lightly over her protruding clit and through the slit of her sex. She squirmed and tried to rise into his touch, but Justin moved one hand to her thigh to hold her in place, never ceasing the ravaging of her mouth around her moans.

After once more dragging his fingers across her hot nub and between her folds, Trevor let the digits dance around the tight forbidden opening of her ass.

She nearly jumped at the impending intrusion. While Justin held one thigh, Trevor grasped the other with his free hand, immobilizing her to his penetration.

"Relax your muscles, baby," he mumbled into her ear, his finger poised at the entrance to her tight hole. Slowly he pushed the digit inside her, her gasps filling the room, combining with the only other sound, sloshing water.

Trevor let her body adjust to his finger, pushing it all the way in as far as he could and twisting it around in half circles, back and forth.

"Oh, my God," she sighed.

Justin released her mouth and allowed her to settle her forehead on his shoulder. Embarrassment pinkened her skin and Trevor could see evidence even on the back of her neck. The sight was so incredibly sexy.

Relaxing slightly onto Trevor's finger, Kara mumbled, "Oh God. That's so…"

"It's going to feel so good, baby. You're going to love having us both moving inside you. In fact, you're going to beg for it again later." Trevor smiled at the slight shiver his words elicited.

After a minute of exploration, Trevor added a second finger to the first and quickly scissored the two digits in every direction, stretching the puckered hole, preparing her to take him.

A much louder groan escaped Kara and Trevor had to grip her thigh tighter to keep her from jumping off Justin's lap. "I need..."

"What do you need, honey?" Justin asked.

"I need to come...please. I can't stand it."

Trevor looked at Justin. "Give her what she wants."

As Trevor pushed a third finger into Kara's hot back hole, he felt Justin's hand against his as he pressed his own fingers into her pussy. Thank God both men had a firm grip on her thighs, or she would have jumped clear out of the tub. She screamed, her orgasm slamming through her. Her ass milked Trevor's fingers as he scraped them against Justin's through the thin layer of skin separating the two of them. There was little doubt Justin was also pressing his thumb tight against her clit.

As Kara's panting subsided and her inner tremors slowed down, Trevor removed his fingers. "You're ready now, babe."

Her body was limp against Justin's. She grew tense at his words. "I don't think..."

Trevor stood and stepped from the tub, all thoughts of actually bathing having left his mind for now. He reached for a large fluffy towel and wrapped it around Kara as Justin lifted her from the bath, cradling her against him.

A little moisture was not going to hurt anything.

Dripping water across the bathroom, Justin moved swiftly to the master bed and lay back, positioning Kara over him.

"Straddle Justin, Kara. Just look into his eyes and relax. Let yourself feel."

Kara did as she was told, which fueled Trevor's dominant side and made his cock lurch forward, begging to be relieved. The entire scene in the tub had only taken a few minutes, but as far as Trevor's dick was concerned, it had been way too long.

Kara placed her hands on either side of Justin's head.

"Lower your pussy over my cock, honey," Justin encouraged.

She was so fucking hot. The scent of her arousal filled the room.

When she seated herself fully over Justin, Trevor reached into the nightstand and pulled out a tube. He squirted a line of lube just above Kara's puckered hole and watched her flinch at the cool sensation.

Justin pulled Kara down to rest her cheek against his chest, his cock deep inside her, her ass wide open and begging for attention.

Trevor rubbed his erection through the lubrication coating her tight hole, grazing repeatedly over the entrance and causing soft moans to escape Kara's mouth. As soon as he was completely lubed, he pressed slowly into her hot tightness and groaned at the intense sensation. Gradually his cock disappeared into Kara's ass. The sight before him was more than arousing. His best friend lay sprawled beneath Kara, eyes glazed in ecstasy. Kara moaned louder as Trevor pushed the last bit all the way in to the hilt.

He held himself deep inside her and lifted her hips with his hands gently to establish a rhythm, focused solely on not coming inside her too quickly. The incredible tightness of her was driving him mad.

~

Kara thought she would die from the overwhelming sensation of having both men inside her. As Trevor lifted her off Justin, her ass twitched with the unaccustomed intrusion. When Trevor lowered her back down onto Justin, he simultaneously pulled himself out of her rear until just the tip remained.

"Oh, God," she exclaimed, loud enough to wake the cows from their peaceful slumber in the barn. *This feels so good. I'm going to come.*

Before she could finish the thought, tremors wracked her body. Both men pushed inside her and held themselves deep within her until the orgasm subsided. Then they continued their pattern of pushing in and pulling out in a practiced rhythm.

"I'm not going to last," Justin muttered.

"I'm right with you," Trevor added. After just a few more strokes, Trevor reached around to Kara's front, between her body and Justin's, to squeeze her clit between his thumb and finger. Kara immediately lurched into a second orgasm making her scream out both men's names, barely hearing herself over the two of them, held rigid beneath and behind her, shooting into her simultaneously as if on cue.

When the pulsing sensation finally subsided, Trevor gradually pulled his still-hard erection from her stretched and aching hole, causing her to wince. He lifted her off Justin and lay down, pulling her between them.

"I think you killed me," she muttered.

Justin chuckled and wrapped an arm around her. He

kissed her forehead. "God I hope not. I'm going to want to do that again."

She flinched.

Trevor settled his hand on her shoulder and brushed her hair away from her face. "Perhaps not tonight." He was smiling when she looked up at his face. "We should feed you. You haven't eaten since lunch."

She shook her head, her eyes heavy. "Too tired."

She wasn't kidding. She was exhausted. The mental strain of repeatedly letting these two men devour her was enough to push her over the edge.

"Sleep, baby." Justin pulled her closer.

Trevor snuggled in also as she drifted off.

CHAPTER 10

Kara bolted upright, the silky sheet falling to her waist, exposing her breasts to the cool breeze fluttering the curtains. Something had yanked her from a deep sleep. Where the hell was she? Why was she naked?

Kara squinted, trying to get her bearings. Memories of an afternoon of sex followed by an evening of more sex with two incredibly hot men rushed at her full force and she gasped. *How long have I been asleep? What time is it?*

Kara glanced at the picture window across from her, hoping for at least an answer to the question of time. The dim light peeking between the curtains indicated it was dawn. At the precise moment the curtains blew aside, a large animal bounded into the room and landed with a thud.

The bloodcurdling scream that escaped Kara's lips startled the enormous…*dog*? It limped slowly back into a corner of the room, its head cocked to the side, seeming to stare straight at Kara.

Footsteps ran down the hall, growing closer as Kara stopped yelling to get a grip on herself. She reached down to pull the sheet over her breasts as though she needed some modesty around the huge animal. It was hurt. She looked closer and could see blood trailing down one front leg and paw, explaining the limp.

Moments later Justin flew through the door and entered the room with another, even larger animal trailing him. When he saw the scene before him, he quickly ran over and took Kara in his arms. Dressed only in low-riding jeans, his chest was bare and even in her moment of anxiety, she noticed his warm skin against her own. Where did these huge animals come from? How was Justin going to fight them off all by himself?

Justin turned his face from her to watch the newest gargantuan pet enter the room as it hurried over to the first and nudged the smaller one with its snout.

Thankful the animals hadn't attacked, yet, Kara shook in Justin's embrace. "Please tell me these are your pets." Before she allowed him to answer, she said, "Those aren't normal dogs." Her gaze was glued to the animals. With a death grip on the sheet in front of her, she tensed, preparing to jump from the bed if the furry creatures moved toward her.

"Those are not dogs, honey." Justin smoothed Kara's hair back from her face and leaned in for a chaste kiss. "Good morning. Sorry to scare you like that."

The smile he gifted her with would have been intoxicating if dogs hadn't surrounded them. *Wait—did he say they weren't dogs?*

Unconcerned about their situation, his hands roamed her back and shoulders possessively. Kara tried to shake the tremors, but she was still shivering even with Justin's soothing calm behavior at her side.

"What...are...they?"

"Wolves." Justin held her gaze steady.

Right. Of course. Like that made perfect sense.

Kara sucked in a breath. "You mean to tell me you keep wolves as pets and you let them in the house?"

A slight chuckle, almost indiscernible, escaped Justin's lips. "Nooo. Not exactly."

"Well, what *exactly* do you mean?" This situation was getting stranger by the minute. A chill ran down Kara's spine.

"Kara." Mocha eyes gazed into hers, commanding her full attention. Justin took a long deep breath before continuing. "We *are* wolves. Trevor and I. Well, most of our staff and several of the surrounding farms are also members of our pack." He paused, clearly weighing what to say next.

In less than a heartbeat Kara bounded from the bed to stand naked next to it. *"What?"* she screamed. *Oh. My. God. He's fucking crazy.* Her gaze jerked toward the door. *Damn. Damn. Damn.* To escape she'd have to pass the wolves.

Justin, too, jumped up and embraced her in a giant bear hug. "It's okay. Everything is okay."

"Don't." Kara struggled against his hold. *I have to get out of here.* Wide-eyed, she quickly scanned the room. *Where are my clothes?*

"Kara," Justin commanded. He was gentle, not hurting her, but not willing to let her go, either. "Listen to me, honey."

The walls seemed to close in on her. "*Let me go.* I need to leave."

Instead, Justin whispered in her ear. "Please, Kara. Just give me a second to explain."

Kara wiggled free of his clutch, but she had nowhere to run. The wolves were blocking the door. Chills from the open window, or maybe from the stress of the situation, rushed through her from her head to her toes.

Justin reached over and grabbed the comforter off the bed to wrap it around her. He stepped to the side, his arms encircling her waist. She could feel his warmth through the blanket. His body temperature seemed inordinately warmer than hers. In fact, she'd noticed during the night as she fell asleep in the arms of two men she'd been incredibly warm between them.

Kara stared at the two wolves in the corner of the room intently. Was Justin serious? *Does he actually believe he's a wolf?* The larger wolf had entered the room in front of Justin and was licking the wounded leg of the smaller animal. The scene was very nurturing, reminding Kara of a mother and her cub. The injured wolf whimpered slightly and lay down on its side in submission.

"Where's Trevor?" Kara glanced at Justin for just a moment, not wanting to let her guard down too much. After all, wolves were wild animals, even if Justin did seem to believe these two were harmless for whatever reason.

"Kara…" Justin began, "…he's right in front of you." Justin pointed in the direction of the corner and Kara froze. Surely he was kidding.

"Wh-what do you mean?"

"Honey, the larger blond wolf is Trevor. The smaller brown one is Nadine." He took a deep breath, and Kara moved her gaze slowly toward his face once again. "We have a lot to explain to you. Would you like to get dressed first? I know you probably feel uncomfortable standing here like this."

"I…where are my clothes?"

"I put them in the bathroom." Justin pointed behind him to the master bath.

Kara tore herself from his grasp and backed into the bathroom, cutting him off. She needed a moment alone. And like he said, she needed clothes on right now.

119

The look on his face as she fled was of great concern, sadness even.

As soon as she stepped onto the tile floor, Kara shut the door, almost slamming it, reached for the lock to give it a twist, and then leaned back against it. Her heart was pounding and her chest heaved. Exhausted beyond measure, she let go of the blanket and slid down to sit on the floor on top of it. She buried her head between her knees and sucked in long breaths, desperately trying to slow her rapid pulse and think.

What the hell is going on here? And how was she going to get out?

Several minutes passed and she couldn't move, couldn't think of what to do next. She glanced around the room and noticed her clothes stacked neatly on the long marble vanity. There was a window, but it didn't appear low enough or large enough for her to climb through.

"Kara? Are you all right? Do you need anything?" Justin's voice jolted her against the door.

"No. I'm...I'm fine. Just give me a minute." *Or two thousand.*

With no other option available, Kara dragged herself to stand, used the facilities and then splashed cold water on her face. The woman staring back at her in the mirror looked like she had seen a ghost...or a wolf.

Could it be true? *No.*

Kara dressed quickly in her wrinkled clothes from yesterday, minus her obviously absent panties that had been ripped from her body. She took a deep breath for courage and slowly pulled the bathroom door open.

Somewhat surprised to find Trevor standing on the other side of the door, pacing back and forth wringing his hands, Kara jumped. When he saw her, he stopped moving and pasted an apologetic grin on his face. He was so incredibly sexy, it was hard to avoid her body's immediate reaction to his. There must have been some unspoken dress code in the house, because Trevor was wearing the same thing Justin had been, hip-hugging jeans. His tan chest had just the slightest dusting of fine blond hair running down the center. Kara's breath hitched. *Now is not the time for lust, girl. Get out of here.*

Trevor didn't know where to begin, but he did know *when*. Now was the only option left.

"Babe, I'm sorry. Nadine didn't realize you were here. I didn't mean for you to find out this way." Trevor reached a hand toward Kara, not wanting to invade her space too quickly and frighten her, but needing to hold her in his arms as soon as possible. He ached to feel her soft body and get back the passionate look she'd had in her eyes last night.

"Where's Justin?" She didn't approach him. Instead leaned against the wall outside the bathroom. *Hugged* the wall.

"He's with Nadine. She was injured. Cut herself—"

"Who's Nadine? And what happened to the wolves?" Kara was not catching on.

"Kara, Nadine is a member of the pack. She lives two farms to the east."

"Uh, huh. Sure."

"Kara, let me explain. We—"

"No, it's okay. Really." She stood straighter, her spine stiff. She wouldn't look Trevor in the eye. Her gaze wandered around the room past him. "I need to get going." She glanced at the clock on the bedside table. "I have a final at ten thirty."

"There's plenty of time. Don't worry. It's early still. I'll get you back to campus before then."

"Well... I need to change, and shower, and..." Kara inched her way toward the door, keeping her back to the wall. He inhaled the bitter scent of fear rising from her skin and arousing the animal within him.

With both hands in front of him, he took two slow steps in her direction, but she cringed, forcing him to halt his advance. His chest ached at the thought she was scared of him. He would never hurt her in a million years. In fact, he would make it his life's mission to erase the look of fear in her eyes and never allow it to return for as long as he lived.

"Baby, come into the kitchen. I'll make you some breakfast, and we'll explain everything." He tried to keep his voice steady, low, as unthreatening as he could. Kara's posture screamed "fight or flight."

"I swear to you on all that is holy I would never harm a hair on your gorgeous body. Please, give Justin and me a chance to explain." Trevor reached a hand out, but didn't step closer. He wanted to give her the choice to come to him.

Finally, after painstakingly long moments, she moved away from the wall. She didn't touch him or take his hand, but it was progress, and Trevor took it as a sign she would at least follow him to the kitchen.

He heard her behind him as he walked, felt her presence, the entire excruciating trip down the hall. Trevor decided to reach tentatively into her mind, soothe her. *Everything's going to be all right. You'll always be safe here.* She jumped, but he didn't turn around, didn't want to blatantly confirm what she would soon come to know as her new ability to communicate with him and Justin. Soon enough the pieces would all fall together. Last night's mating had forever connected them telepathically. They needed only to open the lines of communication and reach out with their senses. He hadn't delved into her thoughts yet. It seemed a violation of her privacy to prowl around in her head without her knowledge.

Trevor and Justin had their work cut out for them. It was too bad circumstances this morning forced the issue prematurely, but just as well. Everything had to come out eventually. Sooner was better than later.

Justin looked straight into Trevor's eyes as he entered the kitchen, a questioning gaze on his face.

"She's very reluctant, but seems at least willing to hear us out," Trevor communicated to explain the great lack of progress made on his part.

Justin scrambled to pull out a chair. "Come on in. Sit." He gestured to Kara with his head. "I'm just fixing some breakfast. You must be starving. We never ate dinner last night."

Trevor had never once seen Justin so flustered. Tongue-tied.

Kara took the seat, her eyes wandering to Nadine sitting opposite her. Thank God they kept a variety of clothes on hand for times like these. If Nadine had been sitting there naked right now, Kara surely would have had a coronary. Instead Nadine appeared perfectly normal in jeans and a T-shirt. Her feet were bare, but then, so were everyone else's. The cut she had received on her arm while running through the woods was now almost a distant memory. Their species was able to heal themselves, and quickly.

"Hi. I'm Nadine. I guess Trev told you." She spoke softly, as though dealing with a porcelain doll. And she wasn't far off base. They had a lot of explaining to do.

Kara stared intently at Nadine. "Hi," she finally mumbled.

Trevor took the seat next to Kara. "Hon, I know you're confused. Wondering how it's possible to feel what you're feeling for us."

Justin came over to sit on the other side of Kara. They essentially trapped her between them, but tried not to crowd her, make her feel as though she were unable to escape.

"*Let me try, man.*" Justin continued, "Honey, we're mated. At least that's what we call it. Sealed together. Forever. Heart and soul."

Kara gasped and glanced back and forth at the two of them, her mouth hanging open. Even under these tense circumstances, Trevor could smell her arousal. Her mind may be screaming "run," but her body could not deny them. The proximity of either Trevor or Justin was all it would take to make her pussy wet, her clit throb with need. All three of them in the room exaggerated the sexual tension. He didn't need any verbal confirmation of this. It was the way of mates. They would always need each other. But the first few days and weeks after mating were commonly known to be intense, filled with a drive to have each other repeatedly. She wouldn't be able to deny the need for long. It would consume her thoughts. Even now, with confusion warring in her mind.

Kara glanced repeatedly at Nadine.

Trevor laid a tentative hand on Kara's leg and she stiffened, but she had to feel the spark shooting between them. He tried to soothe her by rubbing his thumb across her thigh. The reaction was a sharp intake of breath by Kara. She bit her lower lip and almost moaned.

Justin reached to touch her shoulder on his side, squeezing it gently, and she did moan. "What's happening to me?" Her head rolled back, and she gripped the edge of the table with both hands.

"It's perfectly natural, baby." Trevor held his voice steady. "Like Justin said, we're 'one' now. United. The feelings you're experiencing are to be expected. The intense sexual urges are common for our species, but now being mated to each other, the three of us, *you* will experience them also."

A noise on the other side of the room caused Trevor to look up. Nadine had taken over the breakfast duties, and she began serving up plates of eggs, bacon, sausage and biscuits.

Kara stared into Trevor's eyes when Nadine cautiously set a plate down in front of her. "You expect me to eat? Now?"

"Well, you have a final in, what, three hours? You can't go to campus on an empty stomach." Trevor reached for the biscuit on his own plate and took a bite. He was starving, but didn't want to appear to be making light of her predicament.

Thank God Justin spoke up. "Kara, honey, we'll continue to explain things while we eat." He sat and handed Kara a glass of orange juice. "Please?"

"Don't pressure her right now. Let's ease up a bit. Give her a minute." Trevor slid his hand onto Kara's and squeezed, trying to break her from the trance she seemed to be in, her eyes fixed on the plate of food.

"Let me try," Nadine said. "Kara, I know this all sudden, but you'll get used to it. It's not complicated really. Would you like one of us to change for you so you can see what we go through?"

She got Kara's attention. She turned to Nadine's voice. "Change?"

"Yeah, change is what we call it. Transform... You

know…into wolf form." To Trevor's ears, Nadine sounded so young. Of course she was young, younger than Kara at least.

"I'll do it." Trevor stood back and took off his jeans. Kara's heart pounded when he stood before all three of them completely naked. Justin moved to wrap his arms around Kara from the chair next to her, enough to the side to give her a full view of Trevor in the center of the kitchen.

Kara watched Trevor closely, narrowing her eyes. An uneasy chuckle squeezed between her tight lips. *He really thinks he can change into a wolf.*

As she stared, Trevor's image blurred. She blinked hard, but the man before her began to transform. At first it resembled a circus act she'd seen where the contortionist popped his shoulder out of place purposely to escape some sort of bondage. But the sickening popping sounds of muscles and tendons giving way continued, increasing in intensity and volume. Soft blond fur replaced tan skin, until a large lupine mammal stood in the place of the sexy muscular hunk.

Kara gasped and shrunk back, impeded by the arms holding her tightly.

"Oh…my…God. How did he…" Kara's gaze darted to Justin's. The wolf before her didn't move. He lay down just feet from her and stared at her.

Chills ran up Kara's spine. She'd heard stories. Her parents had read to her about wolves and other animals sharing a body with humans when she was a child. But wasn't it all fiction?

"We're shapeshifters, Kara." Justin attempted to soothe her, running his hands up and down her arms.

"You can do it, too? He… You…" Kara didn't know what else to ask. *What the hell have I gotten myself into?*

"I can, yes. Would you like me to?" Justin's voice was low, non-threatening.

"*No,*" Kara nearly yelled. "Thanks, but no. One of you is enough for now." *All I need is two giant wolves in the kitchen with me.*

"*Don't be afraid. I'm the same man. I just have the ability to shift is all.*" The voice spoke directly into Kara's head. The wolf in front of her, Trevor, stared intently at her.

Kara turned in Justin's arms. "Did you just say something?"

Justin smiled. "No, honey. Trevor did. We're connected now in a special way. The bond gives us the ability to communicate with each other through our thoughts. No matter where you are or what you're doing, you can always speak to us. All you have to do is think it."

"What? You can…hear my thoughts?" *This can't be happening.* "All of them?"

"*Yes, my love. All of them. Even the naughty ones.*"

Kara jumped in her chair. She recognized the voice in her head as Justin's and saw the look of lust on his face.

While she wasn't looking, the wolf, Trevor, came up to her and nuzzled her shins. His wet snout forced her to lift her legs out of his path.

When she glanced down at him, he seemed to be almost…smiling?

"*He's right, babe, even the naughty ones.*" Trevor's voice invaded her mind.

Her gaze darted to Nadine still sitting across the table. "Can you? I mean… Did you hear that?" Her cheeks burned to think Nadine knew what sexual escapades were running through her betraying mind.

"No, don't worry. The secrets between the three of you

are safe. Others are not privy to your thoughts." Nadine smiled a knowing smile.

Kara shook her head. *I can't handle this.* She pushed her chair back and stood, head still easing back and forth. "No. This can't be true. I must be losing my mind. Or...or... sleeping. That's it. I'm dreaming." Kara closed her eyes and covered them tightly with her palms. Perhaps blocking everything out would make it all disappear.

A few moments later, when she ventured to peek into the room again, everything was exactly the same. One man with a worried look on his face stared at her from the table. One woman stood to the side biting her nails. And one...*shit*...wolf lay on the floor right where she'd left him. *Shit. Shit. Shit. I've gone crazy.*

Justin took a tentative step forward. "You aren't crazy, hon." He whispered the words.

"You...*you*..." Kara shouted and shook a finger in his direction. "What do you know? *You* are probably crazier than *me.*"

"Try it, Kara. Try communicating something specific with us." Justin spoke softly, inching his way closer to her.

"No, thank you. I'm fine for now." Kara leaned away from him.

Nadine cleared her throat. "I'm going to wait outside while you three...uh...hash this out. Nice to meet you." She smiled at Kara and disappeared to the back porch.

"I need to go talk to Nadine, find out what else she knows," Trevor communicated. *"Don't do anything without me."* Kara jumped at the realization Trevor was still speaking to her in wolf form.

Kara watched Trevor amble over to the back door and nose it open like he did it every day.

Justin crowded his large body into Kara's space and

placed both hands on either side of her. He leaned down to put his forehead on hers and stared directly into her eyes.

"I swear to you we will never ever hurt you as long as we live. You're our entire world. Our destiny. We would give our own lives to protect every hair on your body. Do you understand?" Justin's words were clear and soft, his breath heating her already inflamed face.

Regardless of the complete lack of logic, Kara felt connected to Justin as he touched her in a way she could never have imagined. Was it possible there were forces in this world she simply hadn't been aware of?

∾

Out on the patio, Trevor quickly changed back and grabbed a pair of jeans from a nearby chair. They always kept clothing tucked away throughout their property for emergencies.

"I know you already spoke to Justin, but can I get a quick recap? What's going on? You ran like a bat out of hell to get here."

"Listen, I know you guys are newly mated and all, and I'm sorry to spring this on you, but I wanted to warn you." Nadine's voice trembled.

"Warn us about what?"

"I was about fifty miles from here visiting Melissa. Remember, she mated with Edward from the pack to the south? Anyway, we were at a bar where most of the patrons were wolves from several different packs. I was waiting for a drink when I overheard three men talking heatedly next to me. Thank God the bartender was swamped and it took him forever to get to me, because otherwise I might not have been standing there long enough to realize they were talking about you and Justin and Kara."

"Kara? How? We just mated last night. How could anyone even know about her yet?" Trevor ran his hands through his hair.

"I don't know, but they knew exactly what they were talking about. The one guy's name was Barry. I didn't get the other two. But Barry was a whack job, I can tell you that. He somehow convinced the other two you've stolen his woman, his *mate*." Nadine took a deep breath.

"What? Who the hell is Barry?" Trevor could feel tension stiffening his body.

"I had hoped you two would know. I've never met him before."

"I've never heard of anyone named Barry." Trevor slapped the porch railing, making Nadine jump.

"Anyway, whoever Barry is, he sure stirred up sympathy for himself because the other two guys jumped right on board, ready to come and quote, 'kick your sorry asses.'"

"Who talks like that?" Trevor began to pace across the porch. Anger eating at him. "How could some guy think Kara is his? She's mated to me and Justin. We're completely bonded now."

Nadine backed up a step, making Trevor realize he was screaming at her. "Naturally the whole thing sounded absurd to me. That's why I'm here."

"How did this Barry even know anything about Kara, Justin, and me?"

"I have no idea, but he clearly knew you two had found and shared a mate. And he wasn't happy about it."

"Shit. Did they say anything else?"

"I don't know. I got nervous and tore out of there really

fast before they could notice me eavesdropping. I ran straight here."

"We really appreciate the heads up, Nadine."

"No problem. I know you would do the same for me. I'm thoroughly exhausted now. Gonna go home and sleep for like a day. Be careful, okay? Kara seems so sweet. Sorry to blow your cover before you were ready. I wish the three of you all the luck."

"Thanks, Nadine. Are you going to be okay? Is your arm okay?"

"Yeah, just a scratch. It'll heal quickly. I got too close to a branch in my haste through the woods."

Within moments, she had stripped the sparse clothing from her body and leaped toward the woods, shifting into wolf form in midair seamlessly.

Trevor returned to the kitchen, happy to find Kara had eaten at least some of the contents of her plate in his absence.

"Who's Nadine exactly?" Trevor was surprised to hear the calmness in her voice.

"She's a second cousin of mine," Justin explained.

"What does all this mean for me? Will I be a…" Kara's look of horror sent chills down Trevor's neck and back.

"No, of course not. You'll always be human," Justin explained.

Trevor stepped forward and raised her limp hand to place his lips on the inside of her fingers. It seemed like they connected every time he touched her. She kept feeling a spark through her body in reaction to both men.

Justin ran his hands up and down her arms. "Nadine

didn't just show up for a social call," he started. "She ran about fifty miles to tell us something."

"And?" *Why do I get the feeling I'm not going to like this?*

"And...she came to warn us..."

"Warn you about what?" Tension was palpable in the room now. Small hairs rose on the back of Kara's neck.

"I'm just going to come right out and tell you this. There's no sense hiding it. Someone is threatening us. Someone doesn't want us bonded with you."

Kara was stunned. "How? Why?"

"We aren't sure. First there was a note on the barn door yesterday afternoon threatening Trevor and I, and then Nadine shows up this morning to warn us about some guy named Barry who seems to be planning to come after us. Do you know anyone named Barry?"

"No. I can't think of anyone. Seems like a name I would remember. My God."

A long exhale escaped Trevor's lips. "Somehow he found out about our mating and he...wants you for himself. He's trying to stir up others to come after us."

"*Our* mating? The three of us?" Kara inquired.

"That's the one. I'm thinking whoever Barry is, his is the scent we've been noticing everywhere we go. He must be following us." Trevor glanced at Justin. Kara tried to concentrate on Trevor's words.

"Why would he be after me?"

"That's what we aim to find out, baby." Trevor pulled Kara into his arms and kissed her temple.

CHAPTER 11

Justin glanced anxiously over at Kara every few seconds during the drive to campus. Her head was leaning back against the head rest on the passenger side of his truck, eyes closed. Was she just tired? Or was she so freaked out she couldn't look at him?

Justin sort of wished Trevor hadn't stayed behind, but one of them had to talk to the farm workers, and frankly Justin wasn't inclined to be separated from Kara for one minute.

"We're going to your apartment first, right?" He tried to engage her in conversation.

"Yeah," she mumbled in a barely audible voice. "I need to change, get a few books…"

Justin reached over to squeeze her hand. "Everything's going to be okay. Please try not to worry."

A glance at her face revealed a glare so fierce it would have frozen Satan in his tracks.

"Riiight. You do realize in the last twenty-four hours you've totally altered my reality, right? Please don't patronize me by suggesting I 'relax' while I attempt to process the fact I have not one, but two, new boyfriends; they're both wolves, and a bad guy, also a wolf, is after me." Her voice kept rising with each syllable, until she was practically shouting.

Justin opened his mouth for a rebuttal, but the look on Kara's face stopped him in his tracks. Perhaps now was not a good time to soothe her.

The tension in the silent truck was palpable. As Justin parked next to Kara's apartment and nearly leaped from the driver's seat to escape the confines of the frigid cab, he could feel the warmer outside air rush into the truck. There was no opportunity to assist Kara out of her side of the truck. The woman flung open the door almost before the engine was off and nearly raced toward the building. Thank God the entrance to her section of the condo was outside; otherwise he would have surely lost her trying to follow her into a building and down hallways. She was moving like a bat out of hell.

Justin attempted to stay hot on her heels, but she reached her front door before him, halted only by the fact it was locked. *Good*. No one seemed to be home right now.

Kara dropped her gym bag on the ground and juggled her purse in search of her keys while Justin stood beside her, feeling incredibly useless.

"Can I—" he began.

"*No*, you cannot," Kara shouted.

Moments later, having located the offending keys in the bottomless pit of her oversized bag, she managed to steady her hand enough to open the door. At least when she pushed it open and ducked inside quickly she didn't slam it in his face.

"Listen, I have a final in twenty minutes." She turned in the entryway to look him in the eye for the first time since they'd left the house.

Justin softly shut the door behind him, cutting off the bright sun and leaving them in the dim light of her entryway, staring at each other. Her apartment smelled like potpourri, vanilla if he wasn't mistaken.

"You don't have to stay here and babysit me. I'm fine now. I'll just get to class and call you later." Kara's chest was heaving up and down, her breathing hard.

"Kara… I can't just leave you, hon." Justin tried to keep his voice steady, didn't want to startle her. She seemed precarious at best.

"You're *not* going to follow me around all day. I'm fine." Kara abruptly turned to storm through the apartment as though she'd settled the matter.

"It's not like I'm going to sit next to you in class, Kara. I'll just…hang around outside or something and try to look studious, busy." Justin followed her down the hall and into a bedroom. He knew it was hers by the delicate scent of her perfume hanging in the air.

Kara slammed around the tiny room, flinging clothes all over the place, grabbing books, shoes, papers, folders, and stuffing the entire mess into a satchel. She ducked into a small walk-in closet and returned moments later wearing jeans and a clean T-shirt. "Thank God Lindsey and Jessica aren't here right now. I certainly wouldn't begin to be able to answer their questions."

Justin stood quietly in the doorway taking in the scene before him. Was she always this messy? By the time she finished putting on her shoes, the small space looked like a hurricane had run through it.

"Get that look off your face." Her voice made him jump in his spot. "No, I am not always this frantic. Look. I can't think right now. Cut me some slack."

She was so damn cute when she was pissed and discombobulated. Justin couldn't resist grabbing her by the shoulders as she tried to pass him in the doorway. She was carrying the loaded shoulder bag which slipped to the floor with a thud as he gently pushed her against the wall and lowered his mouth to hers.

The tension in her body eased almost immediately as he angled his head to ravage her mouth. Her shoulders relaxed beneath his palms, and she gripped his forearms with both hands. He hoped he could send some semblance of calm into her system through the bond. It was working.

As soon as Justin thought she was slightly calmer, he released her and stepped back. "Guess we better get you to class," he muttered under his breath. His cock had jumped to attention, but he didn't have time to do anything about it.

"Fine." Her smart-alecky attitude was not helping the situation. Instead of pissing him off as she surely intended, he was growing hornier by the second.

A slow smile spread across his face as he stared at her. "After you." He motioned with his hands for her to exit the bedroom. *If I don't get her out of this condo soon, she's going to find her sassy ass flat on the bed.*

"I'm going to leave my roommates a note before they decide to call the cops. I've never been gone overnight before. If I don't at least attempt to explain, they'll be worried."

Justin followed her into the kitchen and watched her fumble with a pen and paper, her eyes lifted up and to the left while she tried to come up with a suitable excuse for her erratic behavior. His heart swelled. *She's never done this before.*

By six o'clock that evening, Kara was sick and tired of

being followed around by the burly hunk driving her to distraction. She'd barely been able to think during her English final, knowing he was sitting on a bench in the corridor awaiting her return. Thank God she'd been well prepared for her exams before the weekend had begun, otherwise she never would have been able to pass the tests after what she'd been through the last two days.

Later, while she'd worked out with her teammates in the gym, she'd nearly fallen off the balance beam feeling his gaze burning into her sweaty body.

Justin leaned over her form, suffocating her, while she stuffed her sweats, water bottle, and grips into her gym bag. And the more time he spent with her, the more of her space he invaded, the angrier she got with her betraying body. Her pussy was wet beneath her leotard. His gaze alone elicited a response from across the room. More than once in the last few hours, she'd glanced his direction to see the lustful look on his face. Good. She was glad he was just as frustrated as she was.

"Are you going to stand outside my apartment all night and wait while I sleep?" Kara tossed the words over her shoulder as she stomped out of the gym.

"No, because you won't be there."

"What? Where exactly do you think I'm going to be?"

"With me and Trevor. At our house. Your house now, too." The authority in his voice made her blood boil.

Kara whipped around to face him as they arrived in the parking lot. "No. Stop it. Stop everything. Stop following me. Stop running my life. And, for God's sake, stop looking at me like that."

"Like what?" The corner of Justin's mouth turned up in a knowing half-smile.

"Like you're moments from ripping my clothes off." *And I hate that I want you to.*

Justin lowered his chin a notch and stared at Kara, his soft brown eyes peeking at her. He didn't need to tell her he knew what she was thinking. And thank God he didn't. She didn't think she could take the verbal reminder right now.

"Do you need anything from your apartment?"

So this was how it was going to be from now on? He was going to tell her where to go, what to do, and she was going to follow along like a lost puppy? Kara had been making her own choices for many years. She had no intention of letting someone else start dictating to her what she was going to do. She had plans for her life, *dammit*. Plans to teach school and coach gymnastics to little kids.

Kara wanted to scream, so she did just that, right in the middle of the parking lot. She even stomped her foot.

Justin froze. "Kara—"

"No. Listen to me." Kara looked around the nearly vacant lot and lowered her voice. "This is a lot to take in. Twenty-four hours ago I was a regular naïve human. I knew nothing about werewolves. I didn't have someone spying on me. And I certainly hadn't entertained the idea of sleeping with two men." The thought of the two of them staring into her eyes with all the love in the world made her pause. *Who am I kidding? My reality has changed.*

"We prefer to think of ourselves as shapeshifters."

Kara stared hard at Justin, making him pause. Was he really going to argue semantics just now?

He swallowed and she watched him shift his stance. "I know this is hard on you. But, you have to take into consideration someone's following us. Someone's following *you*, honey. I couldn't possibly leave you somewhere alone while you're in danger, even if I didn't have this incredible hard on waiting in my pants."

Kara smiled at the thought of him suffering because he needed her so much.

Justin reached for the truck door. "Look," he began as he opened the passenger door and turned to Kara, "you have two options here. You can either get in the truck peacefully and we can dash back to your place to gather some of your belongings before heading home, or, if you prefer, we can strip down right here in the parking lot and have sex in the front seat of my truck. 'Cause, honey, I am so hot for you, I can't stand it very much longer. I can smell your arousal rushing out of your tight pussy, begging me to take you. I know this is new and awkward for you, life-changing, but you aren't going to be able to deny your body's pull toward Trevor and me. No matter how hard you fight against your preconceived notions of what is 'proper' and 'right,' fate will drive you to mate with us. Believe me, it will ease in a few days, or weeks maybe, but initially, our bodies and souls are going to crave each other night and day."

Kara watched, unable to close her mouth, from about a foot away. Justin gave his little speech as calmly as if he was describing the weather. And she knew he was right, at least about the part about her body. She couldn't stand another minute without him inside her. And she was dying to get back to Trevor also. It had been a long day without him. She sorely missed his presence, or lack thereof.

"Fine." She climbed into the cab and buckled her seatbelt.

Minutes later they pulled up to her apartment and Kara stared at the front door, dreading the conversation she would have with Lindsey and Jessica. The note she'd left them earlier would have driven their curiosity sky high. Confronting them with the information that she was going to spend yet another night, and possibly several, with Justin made her cringe.

"What's the matter?" Justin asked as he opened her side of the truck.

"They're home."

"Who?"

"Lindsey and Jessica. My roommates."

"So?"

She narrowed her gaze at him. "I don't do this sort of thing."

"What sort of thing?" His quizzical expression was genuine.

"Go home with guys and not return." She pushed past him and headed for the front door.

As she reached for the doorknob, he grabbed her arm and spun her around. He smiled. "I'm glad you don't normally do this. You can't imagine how happy that makes me, but you're going to have to face them sometime. You belong with us now Kara. We aren't going to let you go. I know it's a lot to take in and fast, but you know deep down it's right."

She nodded. That was all true, but it didn't make things any easier. "Don't suppose you would be willing to wait out here?"

"Not a chance." He reached around her and opened the front door.

The normal early-evening study music was playing, making Kara smile. She would miss this. Life was about to change.

"Kara." Lindsey nearly shouted at her as she came out of the kitchen and then stopped dead in her tracks when her gaze left Kara's face and trailed higher to meet Justin's at her back. "Oh. Hi."

Jessica stepped out from the hallway too. She grinned, but didn't say a word.

"Ladies." Justin stepped around Kara's side and nodded at first Jessica and then Lindsey. "I'm going to steal your roommate again. I hope you don't mind. She's going to pack a few things."

Kara flinched while she watched Lindsey's eyes widen. Justin had specifically not mentioned for how long he intended to keep her. His words were ambiguous. For the night? For the week? Forever?

"Okay." Lindsey hedged. "Um, Kara, can I speak to you for a minute?" She walked passed Kara, heading toward the short hallway and grabbing Jessica by the arm on the way by to drag her down the hall also.

Kara turned to Justin and set her hands on his chest. "Don't move." She glared at him. "I mean it." She needed a few minutes with her roommates, and he was not invited.

Justin grinned. "I'll wait on the couch." He kissed her forehead and sauntered over to take a seat.

Kara rolled her head both ways to alleviate some of her stress as she headed to her bedroom.

Jessica already sat cross-legged in the center of the bed. Her face was unreadable.

Lindsey stood next to the closet, leaning against the wall. Her brow was furrowed. "Kara, are you sure about this guy? I mean I realize he's hotter than hell and all, but you've jumped in so fast."

"I know." Kara shut the door as she spoke. "It's crazy weird, but I really like him." She wasn't about to mention Trevor.

"So, you're like staying at his place?"

"Yeah." Kara glanced away and headed for the closet to grab a bag and stuff several items inside. "Don't worry. He's…"

"What?" Jessica asked, speaking for the first time.

Kara stepped out of the closet. She leaned against the frame. "He's perfect. I can't describe it. I know it seems fast. But they say when you know, you know. Don't they?"

Jessica smiled. Her eyes twinkled as though she knew more than she possibly could. Maybe she was just a romantic at heart.

Lindsey's face was not as soft. She chewed on her bottom lip in worry. "You've never even had a boyfriend in the last four years. Now you practically move in with the first guy who asks you to dance at some bar?"

"Well, technically I asked him to dance, remember?" Kara chuckled. "And besides, you don't need me around here this week anyway. You've taken over the household chores." She grinned wider.

Lindsey glanced down at her bag. "How much stuff are you taking?"

Kara didn't know what to take, really. She tried to cover up her uncertainty. "I don't know what I might want to wear. And I have practice tomorrow, so…" She let it go with that.

Jessica climbed off the bed and padded to face Kara. She pulled her into a fierce hug and then held her at arm's length. "Call us, so we'll know you're okay."

Kara nodded. A lump formed in her throat. This was huge. It was their last week of school anyway. Things were about to change for all of them. But none of them could have seen this coming.

"Is he that fantastic?" Jessica asked.

"He is."

"Then you have my blessing." Jessica released her and stepped back.

Lindsey blew out a breath. "I feel like the bad guy here. I just want to make sure you're safe."

"I know, Lin. I'm fine. Really. Better than." Kara wrapped her arms around Lindsey, forcing her other friend to relax. "I promise. Justin is the best thing that's ever happened to me." *And Trevor. And God, do not make me eat those words.*

CHAPTER 12

Trevor watched breathlessly as Justin finally pulled up to the house, Kara in tow. After a day of dealing with the dairy farm and preparing his men for the possible threat of some lunatic, he was exhausted and wanted nothing more than to have his woman back in his embrace. Tomorrow Justin could take care of the daily duties and Trevor would spend a leisurely day with Kara.

Kara's firm muscular legs were the first thing Trevor noticed as she swung them around to exit the truck. She was still dressed in a leotard, her sweet essence lingering beneath the light cover of perspiration from her workout.

As Trevor approached her, she gave him a wan smile and allowed him to wrap her in his embrace.

"Tough day?" Trevor angled her face up to his with one hand.

"What do you think?" Kara pushed back and headed for the house.

"Did I say something wrong?" Trevor inquired of Justin, forgetting Kara was now just as privy to his thoughts as his longtime friend had always been.

"You can't talk about me behind my back anymore, boys," Kara threw over her shoulder. She continued into the house and disappeared from sight before Trevor heard from her again. *"I'm going to take a shower and go to bed."*

"We're right behind you, sweetheart," Trevor communicated while the two men hustled into the house.

Trevor's cock jumped to attention and grew thicker and harder than it had been all day thinking about Kara's sweet ass shaking in front of him. No way in hell was she going to go to bed before he had her today.

When he and Justin reached the bedroom, Kara was leaning over her bag, tugging out clothes. She obviously was having difficulty finding what she wanted because several wrinkled items were already spilling onto the floor and she blew out an audible sigh of frustration.

Justin leaned over her and set a hand on her back.

Kara jumped and spun around. She held a T-shirt in her hand. "Will I ever have a single moment of privacy around you two?" Her words were strained, but she licked her lips, her gaze darting back and forth between Trevor and Justin.

Trevor stepped forward and took the shirt from her to toss it back on the bag. He cupped her face with both hands. "Of course you will. Anytime you need it. But not right now." He stroked his thumbs under her chin, feeling her pulse jump with every caress.

Kara swallowed. "Why not right now?" she whispered. She held Trevor's gaze while Justin spoke.

Justin stepped behind her and wrapped his arms around her waist. "Because the bond is too new, honey. We need you. And you need us." He kissed her neck under Trevor's hand.

"We had sex like ten times yesterday." Her throat worked hard as she swallowed again.

Trevor leaned in and kissed her lips gently. "Yesterday. More than twenty-four hours ago now."

"I should not be feeling like this again so soon. It's ridiculous."

"Like what, baby?" Trevor asked. He knew. He could smell her need. He could feel it in her pulse. He could read it in her expression. And he was privy to her thoughts. Right now they were a jumbled mess of sexual desire mixed with embarrassment and frustration.

She ignored his question and closed her eyes, her lips tucking into her mouth. She held her breath.

Justin chuckled from behind her. "Holding your breath and closing your eyes will not work, honey. I know this seems odd to you, but it's perfectly natural for us. That need is part of the mating. It's nature's way of bonding us to each other. It won't abate soon. In fact it will get more intense."

She blew out a breath. "More intense?" Her voice was a high-pitched squeal.

Trevor nodded. "He's right. We tried to tell you earlier."

"I didn't believe you."

Trevor smiled. "I know it's a lot, but trust me when I say it will be much easier on you to relax and let us make love to you so you can sleep. If you ignore the urge, it will only get worse. None of us will be able to sleep."

She squirmed, dislodging both men and ducking out from between them. "I need a minute," she muttered as she lowered her gaze and headed for the bathroom.

A moment later the door was shut and Trevor heard the lock turn. The slight thump jarred the door, and Trevor imagined she had leaned against it and slid to the floor. He glanced at Justin who looked just as afflicted as Trevor.

"Now what do we do?" Justin communicated, carefully blocking Kara from his thoughts.

"Wait." It was all they could do. *"And love her."* They didn't need to pressure her. She would come around on her own. Trevor adjusted his cock, glad she wasn't looking. In fact, he felt like he was suffocating in his clothes, so he pulled his shirt off and reached for the button on his jeans.

"You think that's going to help?" Justin asked, chuckling through their communication.

Trevor turned toward him and smiled. *"It will help my cock be able to breathe. Yes."*

Suddenly the bathroom door flew back open and Kara stalked out, hands on her hips.

For a second Trevor worried she'd heard him through their connection.

But then she spoke, her chest heaving. "Even in the bathroom I can smell you." She shot a glare at Justin and then Trevor. "Both of you."

"Is that…a bad thing?" Trevor asked tentatively.

She rolled her eyes. "I can't think. I can't escape you." She stepped closer, narrowing her gaze on Trevor. "And I feel like you are spying on every thought I have." Her cheeks pinkened as she finished talking.

Trevor tried to keep from smiling and risking pissing her off. She was frustrated. She had a right to be. "We haven't been in your head, baby. I promise. It's hard. But we're trying to give you some space so you won't feel overwhelmed all at once."

"Overwhelmed?" She threw her hands up in the air. "Overwhelmed is when I have two tests in one day and a gymnastics meet the next. Overwhelmed is when I don't get enough sleep and I have a paper due the next day."

Kara spun around, threading her hands into her hair and dislodging her ponytail. "This? This is not overwhelmed. This is way way way past overwhelmed. I have just a few days of school left. Luckily I'm not a procrastinator and I'm as prepared as I can be for my tests. If I wasn't, I would surely flunk them all."

Her voice rose as she released her hair and fisted her hands at her sides. "I can't concentrate on anything. My head is filled with nothing except thoughts of sex. With not *one*, but *two* men. And those men aren't men, but wolves. *Wolves*. Do you have any idea what I'm going through?"

Trevor opened his mouth, but Justin beat him to the punch. He took a long stride toward Kara and spoke. "Honey, you're right. We can't possibly understand. Neither of us can imagine what it must be like for you. You have every right to feel the way you do, and we are both so very sorry to be contributing to your stress.

"Believe me when I say we did nothing on purpose. This is out of our control as much as it is out of your control. All we can do is be here for you in any way you need, hold you, and support you."

"And keep you safe," Trevor added, because right now that seemed paramount.

Her shoulders slumped. She took a deep breath and blew it out. "Well, somebody better do something about this ridiculous sex drive I'm experiencing, and fast, before I pull my hair out." She reached for her hips and tugged her tight sweatpants off her legs, leaving her in nothing but her leotard. Chalk still clung to her elbows and thighs.

As soon as the shock finished freezing Trevor in his spot, he lurched forward.

Justin must have been on the same slow-motion wave length because he moved at the same moment. They both grabbed one of the top straps of her leotard and tugged it down her body, leaving her lithe frame naked and wanting.

Trevor watched her nipples pucker while he wiggled out of his jeans and kicked them aside. Two seconds later, he grabbed her hand and led her to the bed. He sat on the edge and pulled her between his legs while Justin, now also naked, came up behind her.

Trevor set his hands on her waist and took her lips in a deep kiss, fast and hard and full of need. The same need wafted off Kara in waves. She moaned into his mouth, her hands landing on his thighs.

Justin's hands came around her middle above Trevor's and the moment he cupped her breasts, she leaned forward. Her lips broke free and she panted. "Oh God. It happens so fast."

"It does, baby." Trevor grabbed her ponytail and tipped her head back. "Just let it happen. Let us make you feel good."

"So good," she moaned, arching her chest forward while Justin plucked at her nipples. They stood erect, begging to be suckled. And she shifted her weight from one leg to the other.

Trevor pulled her head back even farther, exposing her neck. He closed the distance and set his lips on the wide expanse of sensitive skin.

Her hands trailed farther up his legs until she reached his cock.

He nearly jumped out of his skin when her sweet fingers wrapped around him. "Oh, Lord. Kara…"

"Spread your legs for me, hon," Justin said.

Trevor's eyelids had dropped to narrow slits against her neck, but was aware of her sliding her knees closer to his, and then she moaned louder.

Trevor broke free of her neck. He needed to be inside her. He released her entirely and scooted back on the bed. "Climb up here, baby, on top of me."

Justin's fingers slipped from between her legs, and he grabbed her waist and helped her onto the bed.

Trevor's cock bobbed against his belly. He watched as

she approached, crawling on all fours seductively. She grinned at him and stopped short of the destination he had in mind. Before he knew what she was doing, his cock was sucked into her mouth so far, he lost his breath.

"God, that's hot." Justin climbed up behind her.

Trevor had lost his voice, but he managed to communicate to both his mates mentally. *Holy shit. I can't feel my arms.* He wasn't kidding. His hands lay limp at his sides. All his blood and concentration was centered on the sweet mouth currently sucking him so expertly his vision blurred.

She's good at that. Justin's words sounded like a chuckle in Trevor's head. And then he spoke out loud. "Spread your legs wider, Trev. I need more space."

Trevor lifted his knees and planted his feet so that he could splay himself wider and give Justin the room to take Kara from behind.

Justin grabbed her hips, but then wound one hand around to her front.

Kara lurched forward, not losing her grip on Trevor's cock, her moan vibrating through the entire length as Justin fingered her. "So wet for me, honey. So sexy."

"Join with her. Now, Justin. I'm not going to last." Trevor's words were gritted out. He could barely make the sounds. His gaze landed on the top of Kara's ass as Justin pressed into her pussy.

Justin groaned as he thrust into her. He threw his head back toward the ceiling and held her hips firmly. His mouth hung open, but Trevor closed his eyes again to concentrate on the sweet feeling of Kara's sexy lips wrapped around his cock.

He knew the instant she came for the first time because her suction increased and held him in a tight grip. It was almost enough to push him over the edge with her.

When Justin picked up his pace and wrapped his arm around her, undoubtedly with her clit as his target, she shot off again. This time Trevor couldn't keep from going with her. His cock burst into the back of her throat. And still she sucked.

When Trevor was finally finished filling her mouth, he let his eyes flutter open. He watched as Justin took one last thrust into her and held steady, his own release written all over his face, his mouth hanging open, nostrils flared, lips pursed.

Kara collapsed onto Trevor's thigh as Justin slipped out of her pussy. "Amazing."

Trevor finally found the use of his hands and lifted one to cup her head. "There aren't words, but that one is close."

"This isn't going to go away?" she asked against his thigh.

Justin still kneeled between both their legs. "No."

"I guess I should just be thankful that it's something pleasant." Trevor could hear the giggle she stifled.

"Pleasant?" He tucked his hands under her arms and hauled her up his body, fighting the laughter. "Is that the best you can come up with?"

She shrugged. "You know. It's okay. I mean as far as sex goes."

Justin grabbed her legs from between Trevor's and lifted them to straddle Trevor's torso. He set a hand on her lower back and reached between her legs from behind.

Kara squirmed, her face immediately switching from laughter to lust, her eyes clouding over as she moaned.

Trevor watched Justin thrust his fingers into her, faster and faster. "Is that pleasant?" Justin asked.

Kara tried to lift off Trevor's chest, but he pulled her arms above her head, forcing her breasts to flatten against his chest. She had no leverage. She turned her face to land on his shoulder. She didn't speak.

Justin pumped faster.

Kara grunted on each breath. "Oh…oh…oh, God." She squirmed, but she was trapped.

"Come for me, hon." Justin leaned forward and kissed her back.

"Can't…"

"You can, baby. Fuck her harder, Justin." Trevor stretched her arms higher and waited while she reached another peak.

Kara screamed against his neck, her voice echoing in the room as she let herself go a third time.

Justin didn't relent until she winced. "You're right. That was pleasant." He chuckled as he scooted back and eased onto the floor.

Kara's body relaxed, molding to Trevor's chest as she released a long sigh. "Mmm." She thought exhaustion would surely take her under at any moment, but the men in her life had other plans. After just a few seconds, Justin lifted Kara into his arms, jarring her into a more wakeful state than she would have liked.

"Where are you taking me?" she inquired, her head leaning against Justin's shoulder. Trevor padded along behind them.

"Back to the bathroom. You never got your shower. I'm thinking we should clean you up before we fall asleep." Justin set Kara down next to the glass door and reached in to adjust the temperature. As soon as he was satisfied, all three stepped into the steamy warmth.

The hot water pounding on Kara's skin soothed her tired muscles. Somehow the workout she'd received since they'd gotten home surpassed the one she'd experienced in the gym earlier.

Groggy and completely satisfied, Kara let Justin steady her while Trevor lathered her hair and massaged her scalp. A soft sound escaped her lips, caused not as much from desire as from the feeling of being cherished.

As Trevor finished Kara's hair, Justin released her to run soapy hands all over her body, carefully washing even her most private parts.

"How often do you shave this smooth, sexy pussy, honey?" Justin asked the question with a gravelly voice belying the fact he was still horny.

"Most days. I haven't had a chance since you snatched me into your greedy clutches though." Kara chuckled, but stopped abruptly when Justin's fingers brushed over her sensitive clit. "Ahhh."

"May I?" Justin looked up into Kara's eyes.

"May you what? What have you not done to me yet?" Kara tried to chuckle again, but halted when she saw the serious look on Justin's face.

Trevor grabbed the spray hose from the wall and rinsed Kara's hair, forcing her to close her eyes for a moment.

"Shave you?"

Was he serious? Justin wanted to shave her pussy?

Kara found her head shaking back and forth beneath the spray of water. The idea both scared and aroused her. Words did not come out, but she did manage to stare him in the eye once Trevor rinsed the soap from her face.

Already Justin was poised with a razor and shaving cream. He lifted one of her legs and set it gently on the built-in shower bench. As he leaned forward to spread the bubbly foam all over her mound, Trevor angled the spray of water away from them and reached around to hold Kara against him. Without his grasp under her armpits, Kara wasn't sure she could have remained standing. The process was so erotic.

Slowly, methodically, with great care, Justin shaved Kara's entire pussy, gently holding the folds of her lower lips to the side each time he swiped again with the blade.

His fingers danced back and forth over every inch of her skin, repeatedly making sure he had not missed a spot. Kara's womb tightened with need. Come trickled between her legs to mingle with the lather of the shaving cream and the water.

"Baby, you're so hot and ready for us again," Trevor mumbled into Kara's ear, so close the erotic words sent a shiver from her head to her toes, disrupting her careful intent to remain still and avoid getting accidentally cut down below.

"Hmmm." She closed her eyes and let the sensations wash over her, leaning back into Trevor's chest. While Justin moved lower to continue shaving Kara's legs, Trevor fondled her breasts, alternately squeezing them and pinching her nipples into stiff peaks.

"Oh, God," she whispered in a deep raspy voice she barely recognized, "I need to come again."

Kara held her breath for a few moments, trying to tamp down the desire. These two were turning her world upside down.

"Let it go, baby," Trevor's voice broke into her concentration. With one hand still holding her breast, massaging the globe, he dragged the other hand down her silky stomach and into the folds of her sensitive, smooth pussy. As soon as his middle finger raked over her clit, she nearly jumped.

"Hold still, little nymph," Justin admonished. "I don't want to hurt you."

As though the act would assist her to remain immobile, Trevor pinched the lips of Kara's pussy together and pressed his thumb onto her protruding nub. The ache inside her increased.

"All finished," Justin declared. He set the razor aside on the bench and smoothed both hands up Kara's legs until he reached the apex, currently sealed off by Trevor's fingers.

"Spread your legs wider, honey," Justin continued, setting Kara's raised foot back on the tile floor. "I want to lick my tongue over all that smooth silky skin."

As Trevor once again skimmed his lower hand back up and gripped a jealous nipple tightly, Justin ran his tongue from Kara's nether lips all the way to the protruding naughty little bundle of nerves demanding attention.

All three lovers moaned in unison, their voices mingling.

"You taste so fantastic. I want to eat you until you scream my name and beg me to let you come." Justin sucked Kara's aching clit into his mouth and gently bit down on it.

Unable to control herself for one more moment, her orgasm crashed through her like a freight train, barreling down her body and sending the walls of her sensitive sex into contractions that went on and on.

When she finally regained her senses, Kara was astounded. "I've never come so many times in…well, all my life really."

"God, that's sexy," Justin stated.

"Hopefully we can make you feel good many times every day for the rest of your life," Trevor continued. "But for now, you need to eat and sleep. I'm sure you're exhausted. Let's get you out of this water before you collapse."

Like a precious commodity, Trevor and Justin dried Kara's body, wrapped a towel around her and combed through her hair. The attention reminded her of a movie star about to go on set with her entourage of assistants making sure she was perfect.

"You're going to spoil me. I'll never leave if you keep this up." Kara giggled, but the men paused to look at her, forcing her to meet their eyes, swinging back and forth between each set. "What?"

Justin jumped to his feet and grasped her shoulders. "First of all, we totally intend to spoil you to death every day of your life. That's not a joke. And second of all, you're damn right you're never leaving. Never. Kara, this is not a fling. We're *mated*. Bonded. United for life. Now that we've both taken you at the same time, the bond will be even stronger. We would never let you leave."

Kara swallowed. They couldn't possibly think this arrangement would work. In a few days she'd be graduating, heading into a new chapter of her life. What was she supposed to do, give up on all her dreams, plans?

Trevor came around to the front to address her next. "Don't look at us like that. You'll never *want* to leave, baby. This is all so new to you; you don't quite realize the implications yet, but you will. Whatever dreams you have, we'll work hard to accommodate them. Just...with us added in."

"Come on. I'll make you a sandwich." Justin pulled gently on Kara's hand, trying not to scare her or force her into anything. His thoughts seeped into her system.

"I can't decide if I'm more tired or hungry," she managed.

If she thought she was unsure last week, boy, was she mistaken. Never in her wildest imagination could she have foreseen the arrangement she now found herself participating in.

Kara followed Trevor into the kitchen with Justin on her heels. With only a towel wrapped around her, she sat at the kitchen table and once again enjoyed the culinary skills of her lovers. Even a sandwich tasted like it came from a four-star restaurant. As tired as she was, she managed to eat every bite before succumbing to exhaustion and dragging herself back to the bedroom.

Justin pulled back the covers. When he yanked the towel from her supple body, Kara took the invitation and slipped beneath the comforter. Thoughts skittered through her mind rapidly about the days to come, but quickly were shut out as she drifted into sleep, acutely aware neither man had joined her in slumber. The thoughts trailing between Trevor and Justin just touched the edge of Kara's consciousness, but she was fairly certain they had something to do with "planning" and "preparing" for an attack from some madman. If she had been more lucid, she surely would have asked more questions, demanded to know what the next plan was, but at the moment, she was too close to complete surrender into slumber to care.

"We have to talk." Trevor paced back and forth across the kitchen while Justin headed to the fridge. The two had quietly snuck out of the bedroom as soon as Kara dozed off.

"I figured. I could feel your tension all day, but you kept a fortress up around your thoughts." Justin glared at Trevor, a smirk covering his face while he handed Trevor a beer.

"I wanted you to remain focused on Kara instead of worrying about what was going on here."

"I know. It was tough though. I was torn…sort of. So, what happened?" Justin took a seat and motioned for Trevor to do the same.

"This." Trevor pulled a piece of paper out of the pocket of his jeans, unable to control his trembling hands. He unfolded it and handed the second crinkled note to Justin without saying a word.

Justin began reading.

I'll be watching you. Your time is almost up. I can't wait to snuggle up to your sweet little number and make her mine.

"Wow. We need to figure out who Barry is and put a stop to this nonsense." Justin laid the paper on the table and idly rubbed out the wrinkles.

"Whoever it is, he must be completely crazy to think Kara is his. Does he not understand how bonding works? I don't like this situation one bit." Trevor's face heated as his anger rose. How dare someone threaten them?

"Where'd you find this one?"

"It was taped to the back door when I got back from the barn earlier. He must be hanging around." Trevor shivered at the thought.

"Perhaps we should get a few people over here? Increase security a bit?" Justin got up and began to pace in the same spot Trevor had abandoned.

"I suppose, but I think it might be better if we take her to your mom and dad's as soon as possible. Maybe over the weekend. No one could get to her there with all the people milling around. Seems easier than dragging a bunch of your siblings over here." Trevor grabbed Justin's arm as he passed by and felt his tension. "We'll figure it out. No one's going to separate the three of us, you know that, right?"

"Yeah. I'm just fucking pissed anyone would have the audacity to attempt it is all." Justin took another swig of his beer and set the empty bottle in the sink. "We better get some sleep. I'm betting we're going to need it, and there's a soft, warm, sexy body in the other room needing some serious sandwiching right now." He smiled down at Trevor and nodded to the door with his head.

"Are you guys about done gabbing so we can get on with it?" Barry paced back and forth, waiting impatiently for his new "friends" to finish drinking, so they could help him kick some serious ass. He knew he needed them. He couldn't just waltz in and take on the two huge brutes who currently thought their lives were bliss.

"We're comin', man… Wha's the rush?" The taller fellow —was his name Dick? Rick?—was getting drunk. Barry wanted to get moving before these two idiots were as good as useless.

"You wouldn't leave a guy hanging while his girl is trapped in some other joker's hands, would you?" He tried to sound nonchalant, while at the same time trying to touch a nerve and get the ball rolling.

"He's right, Rich. We should really help the guy out. He'd do the same for us if we were in his shoes." The shorter man, Jake, stood and dropped a few bills on the table. "Let's go. Lead the way, brother."

Finally. They were only a few miles outside of town. It was time to move in and make Trevor's life a living hell.

CHAPTER 13

Bright sunlight filtered through the window, dragging Trevor from the deep sleep he'd finally succumbed to at some point in the early hours.

As he opened his eyes, Trevor stared down at the beautiful vision and thanked his lucky stars. Justin was already gone from the bed. He would have long since headed out to the barn to take care of the earliest morning duties of running a dairy farm.

They took turns with the tasks, and Trevor was suddenly very glad it was his turn to stay in bed and admire the sexy creature responsible for his current state of arousal.

Not willing to wake her just yet, Trevor watched her peaceful face while he ran one hand leisurely up and down his stiffening shaft. Exquisite sensations made his fingertips tingle and he had to grit his teeth to keep from making any sounds that would wake the sleeping angel beside him. He lay back and closed his eyes, letting his fingers increase the pressure building in his balls. Perched just on the edge of an intense orgasm, Trevor suddenly startled when a dainty warm hand covered his and took over the task.

"Were you going to just lay there and have sex without me?" Kara's voice was low and filled with sleep.

"I didn't want to wake you. You looked so, ahh... I'm so close, baby."

"Mmm, I'm awake now." Kara increased her grip and dragged her hand almost all the way off the head of Trevor's cock before gathering up the pre-come leaking out with one tiny finger and circling the slit on the very tip of the organ.

Trevor was sure he would come at any moment, but the pressure from his increasingly tightening balls skyrocketed when Kara ducked below the sheet and sucked him into her hot wet mouth with no warning.

"Oh, God, baby. That feels...so...good." He tried to hold back, make the moment last, but there was no way to prevent the onslaught of feelings sending him flying over the edge on Kara's second pass into her throat. The orgasm lasted forever while Kara gently suckled Trevor's cock, swallowing every bit of him.

When the climax finally passed, Kara lifted her head and set her chin on Trevor's stomach, her deep blue eyes gazing at him above her rosy cheeks and swollen lips. "Good morning."

"Indeed." Trevor chuckled. "If I'd known you were going to repeat that *pleasant* experience, I'd have woken you up hours ago."

Kara simply smiled. "I have to get to campus. Finals to study for you know. I'll never get anything done in this house."

"Yes, but not until I get..." Trevor flipped Kara onto her back and climbed over her body, "...some breakfast."

Kara giggled at the sudden switch. "How can I argue with a giant naked wolfman?"

"You should not." Trevor nudged Kara's legs apart, farther than the average woman would ever be able to, and leaned his torso against her sex with as much pressure as he thought she could tolerate, allowing him to fondle and suck on her breasts while her clit and hot opening were pressed against him.

Kara whimpered at the first contact with Trevor's mouth, and he smiled against her breast, pleased she was so incredibly responsive to his possessive move. It was a good sign because he and Justin would be asserting more and more of their dominant nature as the days went by. They didn't want to spring it all on her at once, but wolves could be rather controlling on occasion and their mates soon learned submitting to them was well worth it.

After several minutes of alternately fondling and sucking on her engorged nipples, Trevor smiled as Kara wiggled beneath him. He could smell her desperate arousal and lifted an eyebrow as he read her mind.

She must have forgotten momentarily her thoughts were not her own. Kara writhed, her hands pressing on his head, begging for relief. Trevor finally laughed out loud against her. Quickly he reached beyond her head for what she was visualizing, restraints.

In a swift easy motion, Trevor grabbed both of Kara's wrists with one hand and pulled them over her head to tie them off at the headboard. Her gasp was loud and her eyes were wide open when he shimmied back down to stare into them.

"That's what you were thinking about wasn't it, baby?" he cooed. "You were visualizing me making you come by force."

Another gasp escaped her and her lips parted to deny the accusation.

Trevor only smiled and reached to close her mouth with two fingers. "Later, we'll teach you how to block some thoughts, but for now, I'm going to enjoy my ability to cater to your wildest dreams. Be careful what you think about while I'm sucking you off. I might have to stop and add more props to keep up with your visions."

"Just…" Kara began.

"Just what, baby? Tell me what you want. You'll have to get used to telling us. Well, scratch that. I guess we're mind readers. You don't really have to tell us anything." Trevor chuckled again at Kara's shocked expression and tweaked a nipple with each hand before dipping lower and running his tongue up from her back entrance all the way to her clit.

Kara writhed beneath him again, forcing Trevor to grasp each of her upper thighs and hold her steady. He wouldn't need a free hand this time. Kara's scent filled the room. One hard suck on her tight little nub would send her over the edge without any penetration.

After a slow exhale, designed to send a warm breeze across Kara's exposed pussy, Trevor finally reached for her swollen clit and sucked it into his mouth. Her mound pressed into him, only increasing the hold he had on her. He created a suction that he continued over and over, flicking his tongue against her clit with each inward motion, until her tremors subsided and she relaxed beneath him.

"Good morning," Trevor mimicked, setting his chin on her stomach in the same way she had done to him. He reached above her and freed her hands with one swift movement.

"I believe so," Kara managed to mutter. "Very pleasant."

~

Kara tried to catch her breath, feeling limp and satiated against the sheets.

A crash broke the silence, sounding like a falling piece of heavy furniture or a table flipping over. They bolted upright in the bed. Before they could cover themselves or move to stand, three large snarling wolves bolted into the room and skidded to a halt before them, teeth bared, ears pointing up.

Kara screamed in terror, and Trevor leaped into the air, changing rapidly into wolf form before his paws hit the floor. The sight was frightening. Even though Kara knew he could do this, and had seen it happen even yesterday, she was still scared out of her mind and scrambled back toward the headboard, her naked body shivering with the sudden onslaught of adrenaline.

Trevor circled the three beasts, his blond fur easily separating him from the two nearly black wolves and one gray one.

Within moments another wolf burst into the room, a dark brown shade Kara realized was Justin when he spoke telepathically to her.

"Kara, honey, get out of here. Try to get into the bathroom and lock the door. Now. Go."

Kara skirted the edge of the room as quickly as possible, but found herself trapped between a large bureau and the bed, keeping her from getting to the door to the master bath.

Watching in horror, Kara grabbed the sheet from the bed and wrapped herself in it. The three newcomers were not just animals. They were people, men. Men who had come to fight. For her.

Kara couldn't even blink. Justin and Trevor circled the

three snarling wolves, growls rumbling in their throat as they bared long, sharp teeth.

The gray wolf made the first move, leaping into the air to attack Trevor. As they rolled and bit at each other on the ground, one of the black wolves attempted the same maneuver on Justin, sending him across the room with the force of the attack.

Kara screamed. How were these two men she was so incredibly attached to going to out-fight three lupines?

Smashing herself flat against the wall, a rumbling noise jerked her attention to the door. Six more wolves entered the fray.

Friends or foes?

Kara had no idea which side they were on.

Two of the enemy wolves turned toward the commotion, glanced at each other, and in a single bound jumped through the bedroom window. Kara's heart pounded. She held the thin material of the sheet against her chest and watched as the newcomers joined Justin and Trevor, backing the lone black enemy into a corner across from Kara. The villain, seeing no way out of his plight, lowered himself on his front legs and put his head down on the ground. Even Kara recognized the sign of submission and breathed a sigh of relief.

Finally, after several tense moments, Justin backed his brown furry self out of the circle and shifted into human form so fast Kara barely witnessed the transformation.

"Kara, stay where you are. We're going to escort this son of a bitch to the barn." Justin grabbed a pair of jeans off the floor and quickly put them on. He then escorted seven growling angry animals and one sniveling beast out of the room.

For a moment, Kara could do nothing at all. She stayed

plastered to the wall, breathing heavily. Trying to slow her racing heartbeat.

Finally, she slithered down the wall and sat on the floor clutching the sheet around her, shivering with fright.

What the hell had she fallen into?

When Justin came through the door ten minutes later, he found Kara still crouched in the corner next to the armoire, shaking. Her head lurched up when he entered, huge blue eyes glaring in his direction.

"You scared me. I thought... I thought maybe they were back. Was that Barry?" Kara's voice was shaky.

"Unfortunately no. Barry got away. That was Jake. One of Barry's recruits." Justin knelt in front of Kara and carefully reached out to her. "I'm sorry. I wish you didn't have to deal with this whole sordid mess."

Kara's chin ducked and her blonde curls covered her face. Justin ached to ease her fear. He gently pulled Kara into his embrace and lifted her into his arms to carry her to the bathroom. He kicked the door shut with one foot and set her on the edge of the tub.

"I'm running a bath for you. The water will help you relax." *I hope.*

"What are you going to do with him? Jake, I mean?" Kara looked up at Justin, her eyes filled with unanswered questions.

"We let him go. He's just some drunk. Sent him back to Barry with a clear message," Justin announced matter-of-factly.

"What will happen now?" Fear radiated off Kara's skin. He watched her shiver beneath the sheet.

Gently, Justin tugged the sheet away and helped Kara

into the bath. He poured bubble bath into the water as steam filled the room.

"I don't know." What else could he say? The reality was he had no idea what to expect from Barry. But now he was certain Barry was the guy who had been following them. He would know his scent anywhere. He wouldn't be able to get close to Kara again, not as long as Justin was living.

"Hmm." Kara lay back in the water and let the bubbles cover her body up to her neck.

Justin moved behind her, tipped her scalp back into the water and then massaged shampoo into her hair. Her expression gradually relaxed.

"Trevor will take you to the library today. That's what you need to do, right?"

"Yes, I need to study. I have two more finals this week. One tomorrow and one Thursday. I have to go to the gym this afternoon for a few hours, too." Kara bit her lower lip, her face scrunched clearly in thought.

"Don't worry about a thing. Trevor will be right there and I'll only be a phone call away. I promise we'll take care of this mess as soon as possible."

God, don't let me be lying to her.

"Okay, but I have a meet this weekend and…"

"I know, hon. And you'll be there. And you'll do fantastic, and nothing will happen to you." Justin plastered a smile on his face as she stared up into his eyes disbelievingly.

Leaning Kara's head back into the water, Justin rinsed the soap from her scalp and then let her rest against the edge of the tub. "Do you need anything else?"

"No, I'm fine, relatively speaking." Kara chuckled softly, but the noise barely escaped her lips.

"I know it's a lot to take in all at once. Two men, wolves

even, and a villain. More than you bargained for when you stepped into the bar the other night, huh?"

"Definitely." Kara ducked under the water and then came up to reach for the towel. "Better get to campus. I have to concentrate for just a few more days. And then... And then what?" She looked at him with questions in her gaze.

"And then you move in here, and we live happily ever after." Justin smiled at her.

"Riiight. And my family, my parents? What am I supposed to say to them when they show up Sunday? Mom, Dad, this is Justin, oh and this is Trevor. They're my new lovers. I just met them last weekend, but don't worry. I'm sure about this. I've decided to take on a new lifestyle, a permanent ménage so to speak. Thanks for raising me."

Justin cringed. "Doesn't really sound like it'll go over very well, explained in those words. Let's just get through one day at a time for now, and we'll cross that bridge when we have to, okay?"

Kara finished drying off in silence under the watchful eye of Justin. Her nipples stood at attention, begging him to go to her. His stare intensified. His cock jerked to attention.

If she didn't get dressed and get out the door now, she would end up back in bed and never get enough studying done today. Justin looked away to keep from grabbing her and changing the plans.

With a soft sigh, Kara finished dressing and ran a comb through her tangled curls. The scent of shampoo filled the steamy bathroom and Justin inhaled deeply but didn't move. He remained rooted to the vanity seat gripping the edges of the chair.

CHAPTER 14

Kara spent the last week of her college days holding her breath. Every noise made her jump. There hadn't been any sign of Barry. Hopefully he'd given up the ruse and left the area. Thank goodness she was able to bury herself in her studies and get through her last two finals. Working out every afternoon took her mind off things also. Lying between two men who wore her out every night also helped her sleep. Nevertheless, by Saturday she was still a nervous wreck.

Luckily her roommates hadn't asked too many questions and had seemed quite supportive of her new relationship with "Justin." Especially Jessica. Lindsey was still leery, but she hadn't said anything outright. They had no idea there was a third man involved. Easier all the way around.

"When are your parents going to arrive?" Justin asked at the breakfast table.

"This morning, just in time for the meet. I'll introduce you after." Kara's left leg was bouncing up and down under the table. She wouldn't have been aware of the nervous jittering if Trevor hadn't reached over to grip her thigh. Tingles shot up her leg to moisten her pussy.

How the hell can I still react so immediately to their touch?

Justin and Trevor both gave a soft chuckle.

"Can you two get out of my head for just a minute please? I have no privacy anymore." Kara found herself repeatedly embarrassed about the things popping into her mind. And the "things" were increasing in frequency and boldness. Sex and its many, many facets consumed her thoughts.

"Babe, we don't *want* to get out of your pretty little head. Half of my good ideas in bed come directly from you." Trevor leaned in closer and kissed Kara on the cheek.

"You'll get used to it," Justin added. "Listen, about your parents... Trevor and I were talking, and we think it would be easier on you if you just introduce one of us as your boyfriend... For now." Justin looked up at Kara smiling.

One of them? She released a long relieved exhale. "That would be helpful, but which one of you do you propose I choose?"

"We thought of that, too," Trevor stated from the other side of Kara. "So we drew straws, so to speak... And I lost."

Kara stared into his eyes. Was he disappointed? *Wait a minute...* She cleared her throat and narrowed her eyes at him. "Does that mean you get to be the roommate or you get to meet the parents?"

Both men laughed and Justin leaned in, twisted Kara's face toward his and gave her a long soft kiss. "I'm the boyfriend. And we would both be proud to meet your parents, honey."

"As long as we're playing make-believe, would you mind not mentioning that someone is after us? I don't need my parents worrying about that on top of everything else."

"Of course. Now get a move on and go put that slinky little piece of fabric you call a leotard on so we can get down to the gym and watch you attempt death-defying acts for the last time."

Kara was in love. Tears welled up in her eyes at the realization they had so painstakingly considered her predicament when it came to her parents. There was no way in the world they were ready to hear their only child was involved with two men.

As for the two men in question, Kara dreaded telling them there was no way in hell she was entirely giving up gymnastics today.

After a quick change from the T-shirt Kara had slept in, she piled her thick hair up in a ponytail, pinned all the loose strands down with barrettes and sprayed her entire head with a stiff hairspray to keep it all in place. She headed back into the foyer dragging her gym bag and yanking on her jacket.

"Ready?" She was surprised to see both men standing at the door.

"Yep, let's go." Justin stepped outside and waited for the others to pass before pulling the door closed behind him.

"You do realize I'm not giving up this sport entirely, right? It's in my blood. It's part of who I am."

Both men froze in their spots and turned to look at her.

"Guys, come on. Be realistic. Did you actually believe after today I wouldn't participate in gymnastics ever again?"

They both nodded, swallowing hard in unison.

"Maybe I could teach a class, work with children. Or, maybe I could train for the Olympics…" Kara kept walking, extremely aware the two men completely and totally bonded to her were not moving, just continued to stand in the same spot staring at her backside. She sauntered forward for several steps with a sly grin on her face before turning back to throw over her shoulder, "Just kidding. About the Olympics, anyway." Her own raucous laughter filled her ears as she continued toward the truck.

Scurrying behind her brought the two hunks back to her side.

"Don't scare us like that, hon." Justin pulled her closer.

"Yeah, yeah. You know you would support whatever I decided. You can't fool me for a minute. Just get in the truck and close your mouths. Flies are getting in." Kara just shook her head and smiled to herself. For all their moaning and groaning about her "death defying acts of lunacy" in the gym, she knew deep down they were true softies when it came to her.

They settled into the cab, Kara as usual between Justin and Trevor.

Justin cleared his throat. "By the way, we're taking you to my parents' house tonight."

"What? Your parents'? Isn't one set of parents enough for the day?" Butterflies fluttered in Kara's stomach. She wasn't sure she was ready to meet Justin's parents.

"They're going to love you. Nothing to worry about. And...you don't even have to choose one of us." Justin grinned down at her and grabbed her hand to pull it into his lap. "It'll be safer there. There're a lot of people around all the time to help us protect you while we figure out what the deal is with this Barry character. So far I can't find anyone who knows him."

"Thank God this is the last time we have to watch Kara flying through the air like a monkey." Trevor could barely stomach watching this sport even after a week of sitting through Kara's practices. No matter how many explanations he got, he couldn't begin to understand everything she did, and he felt nauseous just looking. His fingers were stiff from holding on to the arms of the seat.

"I'm not so sure about that, Trev. I don't think she was kidding around. She may want to stay with the sport just to stay in shape. She may even want to coach kids or something." Justin didn't turn his head to look at Trevor. Which wasn't shocking. It was hard for either of them to take their eyes off Kara.

"So we tell her 'no.'" Trevor gritted his teeth as Kara flung herself from the low bar to the high bar like a rubber band.

"Right. *You* can try if you want, but I don't think our mate is quite so submissive out of bed. And, furthermore, I don't think I would even want to be mated to a woman who couldn't stand up to me with a little backbone." Justin glanced at Trevor.

"You're right, of course."

Finished on the uneven bars, Kara moved on to the balance beam. Trevor sucked in another breath and held it. The only thing worse than the bars was the beam. He hated the idea of his sexy cute little mate slipping and slamming her hot pussy down over a four-inch hunk of wood. As she went to dismount, Trevor actually squeezed his eyes shut for a few seconds to avoid witnessing the somersault thing she was going to do in the air before landing. Hopefully on her feet. He only opened his eyes when Justin began clapping beside him.

"How many more events?" Trevor couldn't wait to get out of here.

"Two. Floor and vault. Don't you have this memorized yet? Dude, you sat through three practices this week."

Justin chuckled. "Weren't you paying attention? You were supposed to be watching her," he kidded.

"Oh I was watching her all right." He mumbled under his breath. "Watching her tight ass, firm thighs, and hard tits poking through the bathing suit thing she calls a 'leo.'" Trevor had to make a fist with both hands to keep from making air quotes and looking like a moron. "Whatever she did in the 'leo' is all a blur."

Trevor sat in silence watching the rest of the events. Luckily the vault was over so fast he could miss it if he blinked, and the floor didn't involve any harmful apparatus meant to seriously injure or kill someone.

Finally, the meet came to an end, and the officials handed out awards. Whatever all those numbers meant, Kara seemed to do well, medaling in two events. Trevor followed Justin down to the floor to wait for Kara and meet her parents. He wasn't at all comfortable with the arrangement, the one making him simply the roommate of the boyfriend, but under the circumstances it did seem like the best idea.

"Justin. Trevor. Over here." Kara was calling to them through the crowd, but her five-foot stature made it difficult to see her, and they were moving against the flow of traffic—people trying to leave the stadium, not head down to the floor.

"Ah, there she is." Justin pointed to her and Trevor tagged behind feeling like a third wheel.

Kara reached for Justin's arm and squeezed tight while Trevor watched in a jealous state. "Mom. Dad. This is Justin."

Trevor hung back a few steps while Kara made introductions. Justin, ever the gentleman, acted as though he had taken a class in "meeting the parents." "Nice to meet you sir, ma'am." Justin shook Kara's dad's hand and nodded at her mom.

"James Shepherd. A pleasure," her father began. "We've heard so much about you, too. Glad to finally meet you."

Heard so much about you? When had Kara had the time or opportunity to tell her parents about Justin?

"This is my wife, Patsy." Kara's dad reached to pull his wife up beside him. Trevor didn't miss the look of affection the man had for his wife. True love. Not something Trevor had often seen among humans.

"And you must be Trevor," her father continued, reaching to shake Trevor's hand as well.

Huh? Trevor nearly choked on his response. Why does her dad know about me? "Yes, I'm Justin's roommate." Who did her parents think he was exactly?

"Right." Her father smiled conspiratorially. "Do you three have time for a late lunch before we head back to Seattle?"

"That would be great, Dad. Is it okay with you two?" Kara looked at the men, turning so her parents couldn't see her face, and made a confused expression.

"What's up with your dad? He seems to know something," Trevor communicated mentally. Out loud, he said, "Of course."

"I have no idea. I'm just as confused as you." Kara nodded in the direction of the door. "Shall we go then?"

As the three walked outside, Kara's mom grabbed her daughter's arm and pulled her in tight for a hug. "You look fantastic, sweetheart." Then she continued under her breath, "like a woman in love."

Trevor coughed to avoid choking. She spoke the words too softly for a normal person to hear, but lupine ears were above average and the low mumble was definitely clear.

From the look on Justin's face and the way his eyes were bugging out of his head, he hadn't missed the phrase either.

"What the hell is going on here, Justin?" Trevor nearly shook with confusion.

"I have no clue, but something's...off. It's as though he knows about us. And I don't just mean our existence in her life." Justin's head popped up and his gaze traveled to the back of her father.

"Shall we go to the Italian restaurant on Fifth Street?" Kara asked as they reached her parents' car.

"Sounds good to me," her mother responded. Everyone nodded their acceptance.

"Sir," Justin began, "My—"

"Please, call me James."

"Okay, James then. My truck is right over here. How about if Trevor and I meet you there, give you a chance to catch up with your daughter alone." Justin reached to kiss Kara on the cheek and turned in the direction of the car. "We'll see you in a few minutes."

Trevor glanced over at Kara as they walked away. "What the fuck do you suppose that was all about?"

"I have absolutely no idea. But I imagine we're about to find out." Justin unlocked the doors with his key fob and they both got in. "Let's stay right behind them. I don't want to take any chances."

The drive to the restaurant was only about five minutes, but those five minutes seemed much longer to Kara. Her parents were acting very strange. Almost as though they knew something. How was that possible?

"Justin seems very nice, honey," her mother began, twisting to look at Kara in the back seat.

"As does Trevor," her father added with a sparkle in his eye she could see when he glanced at her in the rearview mirror.

"Umm, yes. They are." Kara sat on her hands to keep from wringing them in front of her. Her heart was beating out of her chest, and she had no idea why. Something was "off."

"So, what are you planning to do now, dear?" Kara's mom was all pleasant. Not at all what Kara had expected since she'd just told them two days ago she wouldn't be returning with them this weekend.

"Well, I've applied for some teaching positions here in Corvallis. And I'll probably see about teaching gymnastics at a local gym for the summer." Her voice was shaking and she swallowed to try and calm herself.

"Sounds busy. Will you have time for all of it?" Kara's mom inquired, staring awkwardly over the back seat.

Why the hell wouldn't I have time for a job? It seemed as though someone had kidnapped her real parents and exchanged them for the Jetsons. Any moment she half expected George and Jane here to be spirited away in their spacecraft.

"I'm going to need a job, of course. I can't just hang out here without working." Kara spoke the words slowly, as though speaking to someone mentally challenged.

"What your mom means, honey, is we just figured you would be busy on the farm is all. Isn't it a big job, running and maintaining a dairy farm?" Her father asked the question as though pointing out the obvious, rather than actually looking for an answer.

"I guess, but…" What the hell was she supposed to say? She'd told them over the phone all about the dairy farm, but why would her parents expect her to be so involved in the running of it yet?

"Don't worry, dear. I'm sure you'll figure it all out as you go along." Her mother's incessantly cheerful voice was beginning to sound like a recording.

"Uh huh. I'm sure we will." Kara stared out the window willing the vehicle to reach its destination. What made her parents think she was moving in with Justin? She sure hadn't told them so on the phone. Seemed like it would be easier just to let them believe she was staying in her apartment for now. She'd only known Justin and Trevor for a few days.

Finally they pulled up to the curb and got out of the car. As chilly as it was outside that afternoon, the inside of the car had seemed awfully stuffy.

Trevor and Justin were waiting just inside and had already let the hostess know their needs as Kara came through the door. They were quickly ushered to a round table in the back by the waiting hostess who already had menus in her hand.

"Is this okay?" the young girl inquired.

"Perfect," her father responded.

They all took seats, somehow maneuvered into a position putting Kara between Trevor and Justin, her parents across from her.

"So," began her dad, "how big of a farm do you two run?"

Kara placed her hands in her lap and rubbed her palms over her team sweats to dry them. Both Justin and Trevor had a leg up against hers, and she felt her face growing red and hot. The situation was surreal and even under her father's scrutiny, she couldn't keep herself from feeling aroused. Could he tell her two beaux were both leaning into her?

"Relax, babe. I don't think your father is upset by this

arrangement." Trevor reached under the table with one hand and squeezed Kara's.

"We have about a square mile of grazing land and employ ten men who live and work on the property." Justin grabbed Kara's other hand beneath the table and gently rubbed the top with his thumb. The soothing gesture should have helped slow her heart rate, if it hadn't had the ridiculous result of arousing her instead. Right here with her parents staring at her across the table. Her cheeks burned to think they knew what was happening to her.

"A friend of mine actually works on an adjoining property. Stephen Williams." Her dad paused for them to take in this information. "When Kara told me about you, I thought of him. We go way back… We were roommates in college." He looked down at his menu.

"Fuck, do you suppose he knows?" Trevor's brow wrinkled in confusion when Kara looked over at him.

"How could he? He never mentioned it to me," Kara responded silently.

"Oh, he knows," Justin added. "Yes, Stephen is my uncle. What a coincidence," he continued out loud.

"He said the same thing when I called him last night." Her father nearly beamed. "I have to say I was relieved to have someone able to tell me what good hands Kara was in when I spoke to him. I was awfully concerned when she first told us she was staying here in Corvallis because of a man she just met."

"Well, I assure you, sir…James, that we…I will do everything in my power to ensure your daughter is safe and sound." Kara could hear the odd tone in Justin's voice and knew he was just as perplexed as she was. She'd never heard such stammering in his voice before.

"Are you folks ready to order?" The silence was

shattered by the waiter, who had no idea what a relief his arrival was to Kara at that precise moment.

～

The meal continued, filled with light conversation. Justin was sure James knew full well he and Trevor were wolves. Somehow it didn't seem to bother him, nor did the idea of his daughter entering into a relationship with two men, both lupines. Why? Because he knew about them?

As they wandered back out onto the sidewalk, Kara's mother and father each hugged their daughter and shook hands with both Trevor and Justin, a firm handshake Justin thought contained approval. "Take care of our daughter," he said, looking from Justin to Trevor and back again. "And call us, young lady," he continued as he turned to Kara.

"We will, sir." Justin felt the incredible strangeness of the three of them standing here under the pretext of Kara simply dating Justin, when every person present knew there was more to it and none were willing to speak of the elephant on the sidewalk.

Justin reached for Kara's hand as her parents got in their car and pulled away from the curb, waving.

"What the hell just happened?" Kara trembled beneath his grip.

"He knew. It doesn't happen often, but every now and then someone finds out about our kind. At some point your father must have discovered the real identity of my Uncle Stephen. He wasn't willing to come right out and discuss it yet, but somehow Stephen must have convinced him you were in good hands." Justin turned and took Kara's face in his hands to place a chaste kiss on her lips.

"But," she mumbled as he broke away, "they seemed to know we were…a threesome also."

"Oh, they knew that, too." Trevor came up behind Kara and put his hands on her hips, trapping her between him and Justin. "If he spoke long enough with Stephen there would have been no way to avoid it."

CHAPTER 15

Kara tested the warm water in the giant tub. She'd let the steam fill the room while she stripped down and combed out her hair, and then she slid into the relaxing bath and reached for the floral bubble bath on the edge. Maybe the aroma would calm her nerves.

She hadn't locked the door. She hadn't shut either man out of her life for the last week, but she was grateful neither came in to interrupt her solitude.

After a few minutes she began to relax. Thoughts of the last time she'd been in this tub rose to the surface. Her nipples hardened and she reached to rub her palms over their sensitive surfaces. She couldn't remember a single time in the last few days she'd actually been in the tub alone. It seemed huge without the men with her. Lonely.

Kara lowered her hand down to graze over her clit, eliciting a moan, which echoed in the bathroom. Immediately she jerked her hand away and reached for the shampoo. Undoubtedly Justin and Trevor knew exactly what she was doing with herself right now.

And since when do you lay in the tub masturbating, girl?

A soft chuckle filled Kara's thoughts, ending just as quickly as it began. She looked around the room and prayed Justin and Trevor were indeed not listening to her, as unlikely as it was.

Kara rushed through the motions of bathing and leaped out of the water to dry off. She combed through her curls and wrapped the towel around herself to head back to the bedroom.

An exhale of relief flooded her when she saw no one was in the room. They'd left her in peace to get ready. Over the course of the week, she had gradually brought more and more clothes and personal possessions over to the farm. Sometime soon she supposed she would need to move the rest. Her lease would be up in a few weeks anyway, and she didn't presume she was going to be heading out on her own under the circumstances. She needed to talk to her roommates about their plans. They might want to renew the lease without her or get another roommate.

Quickly selecting a light skirt and blouse, Kara dropped the towel and got dressed. A quick dab of makeup and blow-dry had her as ready as she was going to get.

Kara grabbed one of her bags still filled with clothes she'd brought over and repacked for the few days she would be spending at Justin's parents' house. She was nervous about meeting the family, and even more apprehensive about staying with people she didn't know. As much as she had been reassured everything was going to be just great, she hoped the current nightmare, of being stalked by some lunatic wolf, would come to a quick end.

Kara headed to the family room to find Justin and Trevor waiting for her. She smiled and paused.

Both rushed to her side. Justin leaned in to nuzzle her neck. "You smell delicious."

Kara shivered at the slight contact and giggled like a girl. "Amazing what a bath will do."

"Shall we get going? It's almost four." Justin reached for her hand and gave a slight tug. Trevor took her bag from her.

She let him pull her along, Trevor following so close she could smell his usual musk. They must have showered while she was in the bath, because both men had the same clean smell of soap and their own personal scent that never ceased to arouse her.

They climbed quietly into the cab, warm from sitting in the sun, and Kara was glad she had chosen the loose skirt and blouse.

"God, I'm always hot lately." Kara fanned herself.

"That is a fact." She glanced at Trevor to see him staring at her longingly.

Trapped between them, a flush warmed her face at the lustful gaze and meaning behind Trevor's words.

Both men shut their doors, and Justin started the truck while Kara settled back into the seat.

"I'll let her run for a minute." Justin turned to reach for Kara's hand.

On her other side, Trevor gently laid his hand on her thigh and lightly rubbed her sensitive skin. The smoldering gaze she was looking into, combined with the calculated touch inching up her leg, sent a rush of heat to her sex, making her squeeze her legs together in response.

"Don't," Justin softly admonished. "Don't close yourself off from us. We like your legs open, ready, willing." His breath rushed over her face as he spoke into her mouth. She could almost taste the mint of his toothpaste without making contact with his lips.

While Justin's mouth lowered until their lips were

touching, Trevor inched his fingers up to her thong and tugged, forcing her to lift her hips so he could pull it off.

Kara gasped against Justin's mouth. "You can't... I mean I can't..."

She could hear Trevor chuckle behind her. "I can. You will," he said while Justin resumed his now urgent kiss, reaching into the recesses of her mouth with his demanding tongue.

Both men grasped a thigh and pulled her legs apart. Her full skirt ended above her knees, but they shoved it up around her waist. Kara gasped when the cool air from the vent hit her pussy, now wide open. They didn't finish tugging on her legs until they each had one in their lap. She could easily do the splits in any position and that was currently working to their advantage.

The sound escaping her lips was swallowed by Justin's continued kissing. Trevor held her leg with one hand and reached across her to lightly touch her open sex. When she tried to raise her hips up to get better contact with him, she found herself held down by Justin's arm across her stomach. Her hands were pinned beneath his arm.

"Let us love you, hon," Justin muttered into her mouth.

Trevor's fingers continued their torturous meandering, never touching anywhere for very long and never applying enough pressure to be sure he'd been there at all.

Kara leaned her head back against the seat, unable to keep up the pretense of kissing. The sensations traveling through her body were consuming her attention. A tight knot wound up in her stomach, demanding release. She groaned and rolled her head back and forth on the headrest, desperate for more contact with...anything.

"What do you need, baby?" Trevor asked from somewhere close to her ear.

"Mmm." She couldn't open her mouth.

"That's not good enough. Tell me what you want, and I'll gladly do it." Trevor was going to kill her.

"Please, touch me," she begged into the cab, eyes still shut.

"Here?" Justin's voice penetrated her mind as he stroked her stomach with his free hand, not letting up on the tight hold he had on her. "Or here?" He moved that hand up to fondle a breast through the lacy material of her bra.

"Oh, God." Kara felt like she was going to implode if they didn't relieve her soon. Her orgasm was hanging on the precipice, and they'd barely touched her.

"I want to see you, honey. All of you. When you come for us." Justin deftly opened every button of Kara's shirt at an excruciatingly leisurely rate, making her tremble beneath his touch. Trevor's fingers kneaded her thighs, back and forth, achingly close to her sex, but only occasionally moving to lightly caress her opening or circle her throbbing clit.

When Justin finally finished unbuttoning her shirt he tugged the material upward, letting her trapped hands free to rise above her head.

"Hmm." Kara looked up to see Justin studying the situation with a smirk. "I don't think you really need these right now." He twisted the material of her blouse around her wrists without releasing them and used the shirt like a rope to tie her hands straight above her head to the handle on the top of the sliding center window.

Kara watched this with some level of trepidation, her pussy now dripping. Cool air continued to blow on the fluids now leaking in a stream down to her ass. She shivered. They stretched her so tight her butt barely touched the seat and her breasts were pulled up high on her chest.

Justin quickly divested her of her bra, popping the front

clasp with knowing fingers so the lingerie fell to the side. When she glanced down, she saw her nipples standing at attention, rock-hard points poking out from her chest.

Justin resumed his hold on her waist, pinning her to the bench seat while lowering his mouth to suck one firm globe into his warmth. Simultaneously, as if on cue, Trevor stroked one finger gently through the folds of Kara's aching pussy up to the edge of her needy clit.

"She's so wet, so hot, so sexy for us. I'm going to come in my pants seeing her bound before us like this, all horny and moaning." Trevor dipped one finger into her core and raked it back out against her G-spot, an act he had perfected over the last week.

Kara would have bolted off the seat if Justin hadn't been prepared. He simply held her tighter and moved to suckle her other nipple, pinching and twisting the first one with his free hand.

With no warning, Trevor suddenly pinched Kara's clit between two fingers and held it tightly in his grasp. She screamed at the onslaught of sensations. Both men let go and a cool breeze blew across her body.

"I don't believe she managed to tell us exactly what she wants, did she?" Trevor's teasing made Kara look him in the eye.

"Please…" Her chest heaved with the effort to speak. Clearly he was not going to let her off the hook. "Please touch my…pussy…my clit…rub them…make me come."

"Gladly." He smiled down at her and glanced at Justin, a silent message passing between them reminding Kara she was going to have to get into their heads as much as they were in hers and soon.

Teeth grasped one tight nipple, fingers pinched the other. Three fingers plowed into her dripping tight sex while a thumb applied intense pressure to her nub.

Kara shot off with a scream of pleasure, shaking the cab. Neither man let up while she rode out the waves of orgasm crashing through her.

When she finally relaxed her stance, the touch on her sensitive clit caused a shudder to run through her. Taking the hint, Trevor removed his hand and brought it to her lips. "Taste yourself. Suck your come off my fingers."

Gently he pried her mouth open and Kara moaned, not believing her wanton desire to do as he told her. She allowed his dripping fingers into her mouth and sucked hard, licking and tasting every bit of her salty flavor. It was so erotic she never considered the act anything but sexy.

When she was done, Justin leaned in to devour her mouth again. "Mmm, you taste fantastic," he stated while backing off just an inch. "If I could get my head between your legs in this cab, I would suck and lick your greedy little pussy until you writhed beneath me, begging me to take you."

Kara felt her muscles contract inside her core at his words, primed and ready to go again. *How can I possibly need to come again so soon?*

"Oh, baby," Trevor blew into her ear. "You're going to learn to come so many times in a row you won't know when one orgasm ends and the next begins." He paused and inhaled long and deep while his eyes drooped almost closed.

Is he sniffing me?

"This is just the beginning. We've been bonded a week. But... I would expect you to lose all control in the next few days, babe. It happens with all matings."

Kara swallowed and wiggled her dampening butt against the seat.

"Don't worry," Trevor continued. "We'll be with you every step of the way, as often as we can at least. This frenzy won't last forever. Just for a while." A smug smile spread across Trevor's face while Kara stared at him.

Until when? She didn't want to ask.

"I think we should get going." Justin turned to back up the truck.

"*Wait*," Kara yelled. "You can't just leave me like this. Let me get dressed. Someone will see me." She squirmed in her seat and tugged at her hands above her head.

"No, baby. I don't think so. We like you all hot and bothered. No one will notice you on these dusty rural back roads." Trevor reached to fondle one bouncing tit, squeezing and molding the swollen breast. "Besides, I want to see how many times we can make you come on the way to Justin's parents' house. It's only about a half hour drive. I bet we can get about three, maybe four orgasms out of your needy little pussy by then."

Kara gasped, her body shaking with want. She couldn't believe the idea of heading down the road trussed up on display actually turned her on. The thought, no matter how unlikely, that someone might see her naked chest poking forward only heightened her arousal.

Justin drove with one hand on the wheel as though nothing were amiss. She stared at both men in astonishment. "You can't be serious."

"As a heart attack, baby," Trevor said. "And I can smell how aroused the concept of being caught on the road makes you, so there's no denying it." He reached those same fingers between Kara's legs and stuffed them into her pussy without further comment. Pumping them in and out… Over and over…

She shot off a second orgasm and writhed beneath him in less than the time it took him to drag the offending digits out of her core.

"Oh, yes. That's it. Come for me again." Trevor swirled

her come around her clit and moved down past her sex toward her ass. His fingers needed no other lubrication as he circled her ass and quickly pushed two digits into her lower hole.

"Help me out, Justin." Trevor looked at his friend and Kara stared in disbelief. *What the hell are they planning next?*

Justin chuckled, the same low timbre she was growing to realize meant he had read her mind and found whatever she was thinking rather amusing.

He reached between her legs with his free hand and gently, slowly, pushed two of his fingers into her pussy, his palm pressed tightly against her tender nub. Kara, no longer restrained at the waist, writhed against the dual penetration and steadily moaned as both men worked together, pressing their fingers against one another through the thin sheath separating the channels of her ass and her sex.

Within moments, she could feel the tingling, meaning an orgasm was close, and tensed her body. The wave after wave of this third orgasm went on and on for several minutes, leaving her hanging in exhaustion, her arms falling asleep above her head.

"God, that's so hot." Trevor stared into her eyes when she was able to once again focus. "I didn't know you would react so...so strongly to bondage. We'll have to up the ante."

"Ugh. You're driving me mad. I need to taste you. Please, please release me so I can touch you."

Trevor wasted no time running his hands up her chest, tweaking her nipples along the way to untie her wrists. He yanked the shirt from her grasp and tussled with her for the bra now slipping down her arms. Naked from the waist up, Kara gave up the fight and reached for the button of

Trevor's jeans, her mouth watering with the need to suck him.

As soon as she had him free, she leaned in and sucked his thick cock straight into her throat.

Justin's hand on her back rubbed encouragingly. "That's it, honey. Suck him down."

Kara was nearly disappointed when Trevor lasted only for a few strokes of her eager mouth before he tensed up and shot his semen down her throat. She couldn't believe her desire to swallow him and still want more.

Quickly she turned to the other man and found Justin already had his pants open, his erection arching in front of him. He ran his hand down the length of his shaft and fondled his balls at the base.

Kara leaned into his lap and sucked his dick in with the same gusto she had used on Trevor, who was now pressing her gently on her back as Justin had.

"Oh, baby. I'm going to run us off the road." Justin's warning came just before she felt the truck jerk to the right and stop.

"Hmm," she muttered against him. "Can't handle the heat?"

Her mouth resumed its exploration, sucking him deeper with each pass, until he too came in an explosive orgasm into her heated mouth. Justin's hand on her head encouraged her to suck him dry.

When he finally stopped pulsing inside her, Kara lifted her head and stared into his glazed eyes. "You two are going to kill me."

"I hope not, 'cause you're the sweetest thing I've ever laid eyes on." Justin chuckled and the vibrations in his chest shook Kara against him.

Trevor pulled Kara into his embrace, and she leaned against his shoulder while Justin righted himself and pulled back out onto the road. "We're almost there. You'd better get dressed."

Kara gasped and struggled to replace her bra as Trevor handed it to her. Her cheeks heated up and her chest flushed as she looked down at her thoroughly fucked appearance. Trevor tossed her wrinkled blouse behind the seat and pulled her bag to the front.

"Let's find you something less scrunched up to wear. He dug around, pulled out a clean shirt and handed it to her.

Kara pulled it over her head and looked down at herself. She smoothed her skirt back into place. "Oh, God." She leaned her head back. "No one is going to be able to overlook the fact I just came several times in the truck."

"Baby, no one was ever going to be able to overlook it. They're wolves. They will smell sex all over you before we get out of the car." Trevor laughed.

"*No*. Please tell me that's not true." Kara stared at Trevor, unable to close her gaping mouth. "And where are my panties?" She reached toward Trevor, hand open.

"Oh, I think I'll keep them." Trevor patted his back pocket. "I like the idea of you naked beneath your skirt."

Kara lurched for Trevor's side to grab the thong, but she was no match for him. He just laughed at her horrified jerking.

Giving up the struggle, Kara sat back. *How the hell am I going to get through the night?*

Barry stomped around in circles from his spot in the woods just beyond Trevor and Justin's property. *Bastards*! He was growing impatient. It was time to come up with a new plan. He couldn't take much more of this. He could smell her sex even from this distance. What the hell had they been doing in that truck all this time? He hadn't had a clear view, but he knew from his acute sense of smell Kara had come, repeatedly. If he didn't put an end to these two smarmy jackasses who had her in their clutches, she would soon end up with child. Then he'd really be pissed off...

CHAPTER 16

Kara stared out the windshield at the sprawling home before her. She'd thought Justin and Trevor had a large home, but this one was enormous. Ranch-style red brick with a porch wrapping all the way across the front and disappearing around both sides. White pillars and railing were spaced at intervals in the front. The porch alone could hold an entire party. "Justin, this place is huge. How many people live here?"

"Not as many as there used to be. My parents raised six kids here. Ryan, Charles, and Michael still live at home."

As soon as he put the truck in park, people started coming out the front door to greet them. A few little ones ran over to the truck yelling "Uncle Justin" and "Uncle Trevor." They couldn't even get out of the car before relatives bombarded them on both sides.

"*Relax,*" Trevor silently communicated, "*you'll be just fine.*" He reached over to grip her thigh in a comforting squeeze, alerting her to the fact she sat rigid in the seat, jaw hanging open.

Justin climbed from the cab first and reached to lift Kara to the ground. Her bare pussy beneath her skirt was foremost on her mind. *What if a sudden gust of wind lifts the edges?*

Justin greeted the youngsters surrounding the car with quick hugs and high fives and then gripped Kara's hand to lead her to the front door.

Butterflies fluttered in her stomach while she observed the couple leaning against each other who had to be Justin's parents.

"You must be Kara," his mother said in a soothing voice. "Welcome. We've heard so much about you."

"Nice to meet you too, ma'am." Kara reached out a hand and Justin's mother grasped it in both of hers, the warm gentle touch immediately relaxing her frazzled nerves. She was a petite woman, barely taller than Kara's own five feet. It was a relief to find at least one person her size among Justin's relatives.

"Please. Call me Nancy. And this brute is my husband, Richard." Nancy nodded in the direction of Justin's dad who tipped his hat at Kara. He was as tall as Justin, at least six feet and built like a linebacker. He had Justin's thick wavy hair, although it was streaked with gray.

"A pleasure," he said. "You're even prettier than Justin told us."

Kara felt a blush spill over her cheeks.

"Son. Trevor." Richard turned to Justin and laid a burly hand on his son's shoulder before placing the other free hand on Trevor's shoulder. "We're so glad to see you two finally settling down."

Settling down? How much do his parents know?

Neither Justin nor Trevor answered the unspoken questions running through her head. They were too busy greeting the multitude of relatives pouring out of the house.

"Welcome, Kara. We hope you'll make yourself at home here," Richard stated over the roar of noise coming from the children. "Let's go inside and leave these hooligans out here for a while."

Richard held the door while all the adults filed in. Kara was a little surprised to find Trevor taking her hand and pulling her through the entrance. The front room was massive and held several comfortable couches and chairs. A very welcoming environment begging its visitors to sit down and relax. Justin's sister and brothers moved around in the huge kitchen that opened up on the other side of the family room to create an even larger space. The food covering the dining table smelled delicious. Like a true country home. The scene was unlike anything Kara had ever experienced with her small family of three. She had very little extended family and none who had lived close by. Even holidays never had the level of energy she was experiencing in this room. Love and fellowship radiated from every individual.

Trevor continued to pull Kara toward the dining area announcing, "Everyone this is Kara. Kara, everyone." He leaned toward to her to speak in a lower voice. "We won't burden you with all the names right now."

A tall woman who appeared to be in her mid-thirties came forward. "I'm Tessa, Justin's sister. Welcome to the family." She leaned in to kiss Kara on the cheek and then enveloped her in a warm embrace.

"Boys," she continued, looking at first Justin and then Trevor, "how did you manage to snag such a wonderful lady? I can tell right off she's way too good for the likes of you two." She chuckled.

Kara felt her face heating at the compliment. It seemed strange no one cared about their threesome relationship.

"Nice to see you again," said another man who looked surprisingly like Justin. "Well, you may not have noticed me the first time, but I was with Justin last week when you two met at Boot Scooters. I'm Ryan." He reached to shake her hand. "You should have seen the initial reaction Justin had when—"

Justin jumped forward to clasp a hand over Ryan's mouth. "You don't need to overwhelm her with the gritty details right now, bro."

Ryan chuckled. "Later then." He winked at Kara and batted at Justin's hands. Intense feelings of brotherly love flooded Kara's chest. She felt…home. Everything would be just fine.

"Come. Let's sit down. Give Kara some space," Nancy began. "You can all regale them with questions over dinner."

Kara found herself quickly seated at the table with Justin and Trevor flanking her, each with a hand on one of her thighs.

The frenzy began with the passing of a multitude of dishes piled high with mountains of fried chicken, mashed potatoes, gravy, vegetables, rolls, and several other delicacies of country cooking. Kara's mouth watered at all the smells wafting off the plates as they passed them by her.

Before she knew it, her plate was loaded with the best-looking meal she'd seen in a long time.

She glanced back and forth at Trevor and Justin to see they had carefully orchestrated the seating arrangement so Trevor, who was right handed, sat on her right and Justin, a lefty, sat on her left. Both were digging into the mound of food in front of them, having resumed their positions, each with a firm grip on her thighs, distracting her to no end.

With a glare in both directions, Kara picked up her fork and sampled the array of food, mouth watering.

"So, Kara, how do you like Justin and Trevor's farm so far?" Nancy questioned.

"Oh, well, what little I've seen of it is very nice. Peaceful. I haven't had enough time to really explore yet. I've been so busy finishing school and gymnastics this week." Not to mention the men weren't about to let her out of their sight with some deranged stalker after her.

"I know it's been hard this past week, but I'm sure we'll find a way to take care of this ridiculous threat quickly, and then you'll be able to roam freely through the grounds and get acquainted with the farm."

"I hope so." Kara wasn't convinced. When were the vermin going to show up next?

The dining room table was long and wide and it was difficult to carry on a conversation with even the person next to Kara, let alone someone farther away. Kara wasn't used to such a large family all fighting to talk over one another. It was actually kind of a relief not to have to answer too many questions during dinner. All of Justin's family members eyed her curiously, but the food was delicious and Kara didn't want to talk with her mouth full. Everyone gave her the space she needed to get accustomed to them.

She couldn't remember eating so much in her life. She'd been famished.

"Sex and gymnastics will do that to you." Trevor smiled at her after digging around in her brain again.

❧

When dessert was over, Justin's mother suggested they head to the porch where they could relax. Justin led Kara outside and settled them in a porch swing. It was a nice night. He watched the breeze blowing through Kara's hair and marveled at his good fortune. She was gorgeous and sexy and he was proud to have her by his side.

Several members of the family sat casually on the wicker furniture to relax and stare at the sunset.

It wasn't hard to believe after her final gymnastics meet, lunch with her parents, dinner with his parents, and several mind-blowing orgasms, she was completely worn out.

Justin's mother noticed this, too. "Son, why don't you let Kara go to bed? Put her in your old room and let her sleep. Then you men can sit down and figure out what to do about this stalker."

Kara's head lulled against Justin's shoulder. "Hmm, sounds like a great idea. I'm very tired." She looked up at his mother and apologized. "I'm so sorry to be such a bore this evening. It's been a long day."

"No worries at all. I completely understand. And you've had a tremendous amount to deal with in the last week. It wouldn't be easy for anyone in your position." Justin's mother smiled warmly at his mate, he knew the two of them would quickly become co-conspirators against him.

"Come on," Trevor stood and took Kara by the hand, "we'll get you tucked in so you can get some rest."

Justin flanked the two from behind, barely giving Kara an inch between them. Being separated from her drove him crazy. His body itched to touch hers all the time. He welcomed any contact at all, and he laid a hand on the back of her neck, brushing her curls to the side. A shiver went through her, jarring his hold, but he kept his grip and pressed her farther down the hall toward his childhood bedroom.

"You can get some sleep in here, baby." Trevor opened the door.

By the time they arrived at the king-sized bed covered with a large fluffy comforter, Kara was nearly sagging beneath his palm. Justin reached beneath her knees and lifted her onto the sheets as Trevor pulled back the blankets. They stared down at her. Her breathing slowed and Justin watched the gentle rise and fall of her chest as he leaned in to kiss her lightly on the lips.

"We are so fucking lucky, man," Trevor whispered from Justin's side.

"I know. Let's get her tucked in." Justin reached for one dainty leg while Trevor grabbed the other and they began with her sandals. The swelling hard on Justin had held in check for the last two hours grew stiffer as they dragged her skirt from her body, exposing her glistening, cleanly shaved pussy, and then tugged her shirt and bra off. Dead to the earth, Kara barely uttered more than a syllable during the process, which only added to the tight need in Justin's pants. As soon as they stripped her, they gently pulled the covers over her and she curled up into a ball, snuggling into the soft warmth.

Heart beating, Justin swelled with love.

"I know," Trevor murmured. "I know. We'll have to tell her how we feel soon. I think she's ready to hear it. Her mind silently screams words of love to us every time we take her. It drives me crazy with lust."

Justin watched as Trevor turned and left the room, adjusting his cock beneath his jeans as he walked. It was going to be a long night.

∾

Standing around the kitchen table, now bare of any remnants of the earlier meal, the men stared at each other, each attempting to come up with a plan.

"Obviously we need to stay here for a few days, or at least leave Kara here with your parents," Trevor stated. His chest ached at the thought of not being with her, but her safety was their primary concern until they could deal with Barry.

"I need to go for a run and think," Justin muttered. Without waiting for a response, he began to disrobe and headed to the back door, dropping his jeans and T-shirt in his wake.

As soon as the screen slammed behind him, Trevor could hear Justin leap off the porch, his change taking place in mid-air.

"I'll go with him," Trevor stated when each man stared at him questioningly.

"I think it's best." Richard had always been like a second father to Trevor. "He's worried. You know him better than any of us."

Trevor stripped in record time, lumped his clothes on a chair, and ran toward the backyard behind his best friend.

Within moments, he came up beside Justin, who was not running with any destination or haste in mind.

"We will get through this." Trevor knew what his friend was feeling because his own chest ached with the same need to protect their mate.

"I know, but I just want it over with. What stunt is the bastard going to pull next?" Anguish filled the air around Justin.

For nearly an hour they ran through the forest adjacent to the farm until they had worn themselves out.

When they returned to the yard, they silently agreed to cannonball straight into the family pool and rinse off the day's frustration and grime. Moments later, once again in human form, they slipped from the cool water, dried off with the stack of towels always kept in a bin beside the pool, and headed for the warmth of Kara's sweet body.

Trevor's cock still throbbed with the need to slide into her tight wet center, but it would have to wait. He couldn't bring himself to wake the sleeping beauty.

CHAPTER 17

As Kara's consciousness returned, she became aware of the two bodies pressed against her and smiled, remembering where she was and what a delicious turn her life had taken in the last week.

She pried her eyes open and looked toward the large picture window on the other side of the room. It was so dark outside it couldn't have been more than two or three in the morning. The only sliver of light present was the waning moon. Both her sexy men snored beside her. Each had a hand on her body—Justin gripping her hip while Trevor's hand lay splayed across her belly. They made her feel more cherished and loved than anyone in the world.

"We do, you know," Trevor mumbled against her shoulder.

"Do what?" Kara couldn't lift her face from the bed.

"Love you," Justin continued, "with our entire souls."

Kara froze, her breath held while she processed the announcement.

Tears ran freely down her cheeks.

"Baby?" Trevor lifted her face to his perusal in the moonlight. "What is it?"

Kara could sense his concern. "I'm just...so happy," she choked out, "I love you both so much. I can't believe how lucky I am."

Justin let out a breath she didn't realize he'd been holding beside her. "Hey, we're the lucky ones. And yes, we do love you. Get used to it. We'll rarely give you a moment's peace for the rest of your life, honey. You'll find it quite difficult keeping up with two insatiable men." His smile was one of promise, not threat. He pressed her onto her back until she lay between both men, sandwiched against them.

Kara squeezed her legs together, fighting the moan that threatened to escape her lips as she looked into first Justin's and then Trevor's eyes. Their hands glided up and down her body, bringing her completely awake. Her nipples puckered as Justin weighed her breast with his hand and grazed his thumb over the tip.

She lost the fight and moaned. "I'm never going to get a full night's sleep again."

"Nope." Trevor dipped his head and sucked her free nipple between his lips.

Both men dipped a knee between her legs and pried them apart.

Kara moaned again, louder this time. Every time they spread her open like that, her belly plunged with need. She was still getting used to the exposure.

Two hands landed on her thighs and smoothed up to her center until both men teased her slit at the same time. When they both pressed a finger into her, stretching her pussy open, she nearly screamed. Her eyes shot open wide, and she bit her lower lip. She squirmed to escape their grip, as if that were possible. "We can't do this," she hissed. "Not here. Not in your parents' house. Justin…"

Justin chuckled into her ear and nibbled a path down her neck. "Honey, no one can hear us. We're the only ones on this wing of the house right now. Besides, they all know what we're doing."

Her face flamed at the idea. She gripped both men by the arms and pushed. "God. That makes me feel even worse. I don't want your parents to think we're having sex under their roof."

Trevor laughed this time, but the intrusion in her tight core disappeared. He smoothed his hand up her body until he stroked her cheek and drew her face to his. "Kara, we *are* having sex under their roof. And there's no way to avoid it. Newly mated wolves and their partners don't know the meaning of control. It's understood. Expected."

She wiggled some more, feeling the heat run from her face to her chest. "Well, I'm not a wolf. I'm human. And humans don't have sex in their parents' house."

Justin and Trevor held her legs firmer with their knees to keep her from squirming away.

Kara panted, frustrated with the need consuming her as fingers reached back into her pussy from both men.

Justin kissed her open mouth. "If you're concerned, try not to squeal so loudly, hon."

Kara pursed her lips. She set a hand on each shoulder, but there was no stopping them from torturing her. And she couldn't deny the torment was delicious. Her clit pulsed with the need to be touched while her men lazily thrust in and out of her with their fingers. The stretch made her brain scramble. She couldn't keep the noises from escaping her mouth.

Suddenly their thumbs landed on both sides of her clit and rolled it between them.

Kara came hard, her pussy pulsing around the intrusion, her clit throbbing in rhythm. She dug her nails into two shoulders and fought against the scream that wanted to fill the quiet dead of night.

Her ears were ringing as she came down from her high. Her chest pounded. Both men continued to caress her until she flinched from the sensitivity. Before she climbed back to a fully aroused state, they released her.

"You're so sexy when you come, baby." Trevor kissed her cheek. "I'll never get enough of watching you."

Justin kissed her other cheek. He cupped her breast and stroked the underside with his fingers. "I love the way your nipples pebble even when we aren't touching them." He leaned down and flicked his tongue over one to emphasize his point.

Trevor pulled the blankets back up over them and settled on the pillow beside her. "Sleep, baby. There's still a few hours before daylight."

She squirmed. Her body was nowhere near sated. And two huge legs still held her open.

"Mmm," Justin muttered on her other side as he too relaxed into the pillow. "Stop wiggling so much. You're body needs a rest. If you can't keep still, we won't be able to resist your sweet body." He set a hand on her belly and pressed.

Sleep? Now? With them holding her open, their hands skimmed her body, their breath heating her neck on both sides?

Trevor chuckled. "Yes, baby. Sleep." He leaned closer and kissed her earlobe. "Love you."

Justin did the same on his side. "So much."

It seem preposterous, but eventually she settled as their breathing steadied on each side of her. She took long deep breaths.

With warm thoughts of love flitting through her mind, Kara once again closed her eyes and let herself fall into a deep dreamless sleep, slowly losing conscious awareness of the two lovers worshipping her with their stroking hands on each side of her.

~

"Can't you two get your act together?" Barry paced nervously around the hotel room. "That's my woman those bastards are violating. Are you going to help me go get her or sit around here like a couple of pansies?"

Rich and Jake looked up from hovering over the pizza box. The TV was blaring some game show and getting on Barry's last nerve.

"Dude, I don't know about this plan of yours," Jake started. "Last time we followed your plan, six wolves pounced us. We barely escaped with our lives."

Barry was exasperated. "Are you still whining about getting caught by those wusses? It isn't our fault you didn't jump ship with us. I had no way of knowing those other wolves were going to join the fray."

"I'm just saying…" Jake took another bite of pizza. All these guys ever did was eat and drink and spend the money Barry didn't have much of. "Those dudes were pissed. I was lucky they let me go at all."

"See, it just goes to show you they have no balls."

"Yeah, well, in any case, they were pretty clear about what they intended to do with *your* balls if you didn't back off." Jake chuckled at his own pun.

"I'm not worried about those two. Look, we have it all worked out this time. I told you, Justin and Trevor took Kara to their parents' house. My plan is foolproof. Are you gonna help a guy when he's down or not? It's like they're holding her hostage."

"Of course we are, man." Rich spoke with his mouth full and then used his sleeve to wipe pizza sauce off his lips. "You'd do it for us, right?"

"That's the spirit. Now finish up so we can get going. I want to be at their place in the wee hours of the morning, setting our trap." Barry clapped his hands in front of him and tried to make his little pep talk sound inspiring. These losers were beginning to wear on him, but they were the only losers he had, and right now any help was better than no help at all.

CHAPTER 18

Justin followed Trevor out of the room early the next morning, softly closing the door behind him. Neither of them could sleep. "Man, I love that woman."

Trevor only chuckled.

They'd only been asleep a few hours, but Justin was itching to go check on their property. Something didn't seem right.

When they entered the kitchen, Justin immediately noticed an air of tension. His father stood at the counter drinking a cup of coffee with a furrowed brow. His three brothers, Ryan, Charles, and Michael sat around the table, as well as Stephen Williams, Justin's uncle, who he now knew was a friend of Kara's father. They all looked up at once and Stephen stood. "Justin. Trevor." He reached to shake their hands.

After quick formalities, Justin began. "What's going on?" His brothers looked wiggly and concerned. Did someone drag them out of bed?

"Your father called a few days ago," Stephen motioned toward where Richard Masters leaned against the counter, "to fill me in on the threats you've been receiving. I've been keeping an eye on your property since you two headed out here last night, at least the eastern side."

"Thanks, man. We appreciate any help we can get at this point." Trevor ran his hands through his tousled hair in a gesture Justin was used to seeing. His signature move of frustration.

"I know you've found a mate. I spoke with Kara's father last week. He and I have been friends since college. He... knows." Stephen paused.

"So we gathered," Justin began, "when we met him Sunday. Clearly he wasn't in the dark about us."

"Anyway," Stephen continued, "early this morning before dawn one of my men came to tell me he saw a few wolves wandering around in the woods between our properties, staking things out. He didn't confront them, as he was alone at the time, but he did say he'd seen one of them in the woods before." Stephen scrunched his eyes and his lips thinned in anger.

"I can't believe how bold this guy is. Does he actually think he could win in a duel against the two of us?" Justin began to pace.

His father stepped forward and set down the cup of coffee he was nursing. "There's more."

Justin froze and turned to stare at his father. His tone was menacing.

"Sit. Both of you." Richard Masters was serious. He motioned to both Trevor and Justin as he took his own seat at the head of the table. "There are...things you don't know. Things you need to know. All of you." Justin's father looked pointedly around the table while Trevor and Justin took the unoccupied chairs.

"Richard," Stephen began, "let me."

His father nodded and wrapped his hands around his coffee.

Justin held his breath and waited, a fine layer of sweat forming on his forehead. What the hell was going on?

"We figured out who Barry is." Stephen spoke in a firm voice and leaned forward on his elbows. "Bartholomew Welsh."

"Who the hell is he? Never heard of him." Justin couldn't help but interrupt.

"I know, and that's our fault. We, your father and the rest of the elders, thought it best. At the time. There was no reason to upset you." Stephen paused and took a breath.

"Upset me about what?" Justin wanted to scream. The tension in the room was thick. For once, his brothers were all silent.

"Not *you*, so much as Trevor." Stephen turned to face Trevor. "This is about your parents."

"My parents? What about them? They died in an accident, right? When I was five." Trevor glanced at Justin with fear in his eyes. *"Do you know what this is about?"* he silently spoke through the bond.

Justin could only shake his head and return his attention to Stephen.

"Not really an accident, no. As you know, your father was a physician. And your mother was a nurse. They were quite a team and very helpful to our kind. Any time someone in the pack needed medical attention, they were always there. You know it's nearly impossible for us to seek outside medical help and keep our race a secret."

"Of course. What happened to them?" Trevor's impatience for Stephen to get on with the story was evident in his tone.

"Mind you, this was twenty-three years ago. Our pack didn't yet own quite as much land as we do now. There was a lot of surrounding land other packs and lone wolves occupied in the area." Stephen cleared his throat and continued. "One such family was Barry's. His mother and father, Betty and Bartholomew Welsh, lived on a patch of land several miles from here with no connection to any particular pack. One night, about two o'clock in the morning, a young man, Barry as it turns out, showed up at your parents' house pounding on the door."

"I remember it. I remember the pounding and the screaming. I'd forgotten." Trevor stared straight at Stephen and Justin ached for the little boy who'd endured whatever the rest of the story would entail.

"It wasn't completely unusual. After all, your father was a doctor. Dr. John Shields. It happened from time to time. When he let the young fellow in, he could barely understand him. Barry was scared. He managed to tell your parents his mom was in labor at home and his dad didn't have the money to pay for help, so he hadn't intended to take her to a hospital. But something was wrong and his mom had been screaming for several hours. Barry didn't think it was right. He had snuck out and come to get the doctor. Ran all the way in human form. Not thinking of anything but getting someone to help his mom.

"Of course your parents hurried to get over there," Stephen continued to address Trevor. "They were afraid your mother might be needed too, so they dropped you off here with Richard and Nancy, and headed to the small farmhouse. We know everything I just told you from the quick explanation John gave before they left.

"What happened next is not as certain, but we did manage to piece together most of the story." Stephen stood and walked over to the counter to refill his coffee. After taking a slow sip, he sat back down. No one spoke. No one breathed it seemed. Justin stared around the table at the wide eyes of all his brothers and the troubled gaze of his best friend.

"John and Mary took Bartholomew Jr., Barry, with them back to his place, but he apparently ran off when they arrived, not wanting to hear any more of his mother's screaming. He was only fifteen at the time. It would have been very traumatic for such a young man."

Stephen lifted his head. "Hours later when Dr. Shields and Mary didn't return, Richard called the police who arrived on the scene to find a hostage situation.

"Barry's father was screaming and waving around a gun. Apparently he was quite crazed. His wife must have already died before John and Mary arrived. And the baby, too. It was a breach birth. She'd lost too much blood. John tried desperately to convince Bart nothing could be done for his wife. Barry's father, however, demanded John 'fix' his wife and child. John was unable to calm the crazed man and obviously unable to bring his wife back to life, so Bart, the older Bartholomew, shot them both and then turned the gun on himself."

"Oh my God." Trevor shook his head back and forth. Justin reached over to place his hand on his friend's arm.

"So," Justin began, "are we to believe this fifteen-year-old kid is all grown up now and seeking revenge against Trevor for the supposed crimes of his parents? He thinks it's their fault his family is dead?"

"That would be my guess," Stephen stated.

Richard coughed. "I'm guessing he wants to hurt Trevor like he's been hurt, by going after his bondmate and you." He looked pointedly at Justin.

"What should we do now?" Justin looked at his father before turning his gaze to Stephen. Their input would be his most valued asset.

His father stood and headed over to the counter.

Moments later he returned with a map of the area and spread it out on the table.

Ryan spoke up and stood to peer over the map. "We split up. Search the area. There are many of us and only a few of them. We know they're in the area. Uncle Stephen's men just saw them this morning."

"I'll go with Ryan," Charles said.

"You boys are right." Richard motioned to the youngest Masters. "Michael, you come with me. Justin, you with Stephen. Trevor, you stay here. The women aren't even up yet. Let's head out in pairs and scout the area until we find something. We'll meet back here in two hours. Sound good?"

Stephen reached to begin removing his shirt. "I'll stop by the barn and set up several other groups to scout the area."

Justin paused before heading out the door and glanced back at Trevor. "We'll find him, man. Trust me. This will all get worked out."

Barry stopped in his tracks and reached out to grab his cohorts. "It's time. Surely someone has caught our scent by now. Stick to the plan. We're going to shift and then I want you two to wander around looking like you're staking the place out for another hour after I leave, then you can both cut out and we'll meet back at the hotel."

"How is this gonna work again?" Jake was dumber than a barn.

"It's a decoy, man. Shit. Don't you know anything?" Chances were Rich didn't know what he was talking about either, but he looked awfully smug with his big word "decoy."

"Like a fake duck when huntin'?" Jake smiled like he'd just discovered America.

"Something like that, sure." Barry was losing his patience. "Just do as I said."

"Where will you be, man?"

"Grabbing the prize. The spoils of war, so to speak." Barry couldn't help but pump out his chest a little at the thought.

"And what's in it for us?"

"Yeah, man, what's in it for us?" Jake echoed.

Barry beamed. "You get to stay with the blonde at the hotel while I go finish up the job."

"Awesome." Rich grinned. "Can we, you know, mess with her a little bit?"

"Not a fucking chance, dude. Hands off." No way was Barry going to let these varmints touch his prize. "Your job is to guard her."

"Well, shit." Jake threw his hunting hat down on the floor. "That ain't no fun. How is we benefittin' from this?"

Barry threw in the piece de resistance. "She has friends, man. Roommates. Two of them. Hot chicks, too. I'm sure she'll set you both up once she's rescued from hell. She'll be so grateful for all we've done for her; she'll do anything to show her thanks."

"Awesome. We're on it. You can count on us." Jake reached down to grab his hat.

I sure hope so.

Trevor paced the front room of the house waiting on word from the men. It was early. Nancy had wandered into the kitchen and made more coffee for him while he caught her up on everything happening. Of course she knew the story of Bartholomew, but she hadn't been aware of this morning's development.

"Trevor," Nancy said in a calming voice. "Relax. They'll find him."

"I know. I just hate waiting here doing nothing. I should have gone with them." Trevor wrung his hands in front of him and continued his pacing. His stomach was in knots. A crazy man had threatened his new family. His best friend and his woman. And here he stood doing nothing.

A piercing scream tore through the air. *Kara*. God almighty. Trevor ran through the living room and down the hall. Fear climbed up his spine. If anything happened to her…

When he came to a stop in front of the room he'd shared with her just an hour ago, he found the door locked. "Kara?"

Silence met him, but he could still smell her. His mate.

Adrenaline pumping, Trevor stood back and then rammed the door, shattering the frame as the wood buckled and fell into the room.

Nothing. The window stood wide open, the curtain fluttering in the breeze.

Trevor could hear Nancy and Tessa screaming behind him, but he wasted no time. He ran for the open window, shifting midair and bounding through it toward the ground. He couldn't be more than a few seconds behind them. Where were they?

Justin had taken off at a run with Stephen on his heels. They'd moved at a breakneck pace to reach the farmhouse in attempt to catch the roving wolves trespassing on his property.

Anger pressed Justin on faster and faster. He paused every now and then to raise his snout into the air, but found no trace of scent indicating any other shifters were in the area. After circling the property in a spiral, the two stopped to catch their breath.

"No one's here, man. They must've left. We better swing back to your dad's place and check in." Stephen turned away to get started.

"Wait," Justin cleared his head to listen. *"Fuck! Trevor? Where are you? What happened?"*

Trevor was screaming at Justin through their connection. The bond was even tighter since they had mated. Justin could not only "hear" what Trevor was communicating, but also feel his fear, his anxiety. In fact, he'd sensed it a moment before Trevor had spoken.

"He's got her."

Justin began running as fast as possible even before Trevor finished his thought.

Kara had bolted upright from a deep sleep. What time was it? A glance at the window told her it was morning. Her skin crawled. The hair on her arms stood on end. Something wasn't right. It was eerily quiet. She grabbed Justin's T-shirt and pulled it over her head.

A shuffling noise yanked Kara's gaze toward the dark shadows on the far side of the room. Suddenly, a man she'd never seen before materialized into view. He was wearing only jeans, his short spiky black hair poking up at all angles from his head in a manner suggesting it was his style rather than causing her to believe he'd just risen from bed. Dark evil eyes penetrated her. They seemed almost hypnotizing.

Kara screamed as loud as she could and backed away from the stranger. *This must be Barry.*

She was far too small to outsmart him though. Rough fingers reached out to rasp against Kara's bare arm and yank her into his embrace. He quickly covered her mouth with his vile hand and then stuffed a cloth of some sort between her open lips just as she was attempting to bite him. Panic filled her. She kicked and wriggled to free herself from his clutches. To no avail. He was way too large.

An angry snarl followed. "Stop this instant," he demanded. "You will obey *me* now instead of those loathsome creatures you've been cavorting with. Do you understand?"

He didn't wait for a response, but snatched her up and jumped through the window.

Where was everyone? There was no way they would have willingly left her alone in the house. Renewed fear made her blood boil. What if he'd hurt or killed them? Had this attacker gotten to them first?

Fear shook her to the bone. *No.* She should never let an attacker take her to another location.

Kara, you're strong. Fight.

Struggling with all her might, she kicked the man and slammed her head into her attacker's face. He had such a tight grip on her though, and she was no match for someone his size.

"Kara. It's Trevor. I'm right behind you." Trevor's voice reached into her panicked mind.

"Trevor?"

"If you can get free of him, I can take him out. I'm in wolf form. I don't have a weapon. I don't want to hurt you."

The madman was still running toward the tree line with Kara in his clutches. *Think, Kara…* A moment later,

Kara twisted her body and slammed her knee into his groin.

Nasty breath flew into her face as her attacker paused before losing his grip on her just enough to allow her to scramble from his clutches.

The moment she hit the ground, falling hard on her butt, she caught the blur of motion that could only be Trevor flying through the air over her to pounce into the jackass holding his balls.

She expected to watch the huge blond wolf who was now a part of her slam into the human and maul him to death. But at the last second, where only a moment ago stood a man running with her in his arms, a gray wolf appeared, and now a snarling fight ensued making her scramble backward for her life. *"Trevor,"* she screamed. Fear for his safety made her blood boil anew.

"Kara, get back." Justin's voice mingled with Kara's thoughts for a moment before she realized he was speaking to her. She looked around frantically and saw him standing several yards away, a rifle aimed at the duo battling on the ground like two lion cubs. *"Trevor,"* Justin continued, *"give me a shot here, man. I don't want to have to nurse your sorry ass if you don't get out of the way long enough for me to shoot this bastard."*

Kara turned her gaze back toward Trevor just in time to see him let go of his hold on her attacker and jump back. The element of surprise was on their side she realized. No one would have been privy to their conversation but the three of them.

Seconds later an ear-piercing shot rang out, knocking the gray wolf to the ground in a heap of silence.

Kara felt rather than saw Justin rushing up behind her. She couldn't pull her gaze away from the dead wolf. Tears poured down her face and she began to sob. Her ass hurt from her fall to the ground. Warm hands gathered her up and lifted her into an embrace she would never take for granted.

"You're bleeding," Justin mumbled. Kara followed his gaze to her feet.

"I can't even feel it." Sure enough her heels were all scraped up from scrambling across the rugged ground. "It's just a scratch, I'm sure."

"Baby." Trevor now wrapped his naked self into the threesome and Kara looked up once again to find the two loves of her life leaning head to head snuggling her between them.

"It's over?"

"Yeah, hon, it's most definitely over. Let's go home."

EPILOGUE

Two months later…

Kara awoke one morning to find herself once again alone in an empty bed for the third time that week.

"Trevor? Justin?" Calling out to them in the morning through their bond was becoming a habit for her.

"Yeah, babe? We're in the barn." Trevor reached out to her mind.

"We'll be back in a few. There's breakfast in the kitchen warming on the stove," Justin added.

Kara dragged her lazy self out of bed and pulled a T-shirt over her head. She meandered toward the kitchen only because she was starving, not because she felt energetic.

What the hell is the matter with me? All I do is sleep. Kara figured after all she'd been through, not to mention four years of college, studying and working out day after day, her body needed a break. She was exhausted. But this was getting ridiculous.

She'd fully intended to spend the summer teaching gymnastics at a local gym, but the idea never fully materialized. She'd worked hard on the farm at first, learning everything about a dairy. And then she'd started sleeping too much. It seemed all she ever did was sleep and have sex.

Neither man mentioned the fact that she hadn't gotten a job at all. Even though they had convinced her not to take a teaching job for the fall, and she'd withdrawn her applications, that hadn't been a difficult decision. Getting used to all the changes in her life had taken precedence. Starting a career at the same time would have pushed her over the edge.

And now, with all the sleeping she did, she couldn't imagine how she would have managed. School would start in a few weeks. She was in no condition to get up every morning and go to work.

She told herself it was all the changes that drove her to exhaustion. Satisfying two men and their insatiable appetites for her body was monumental. Learning an entire different way of life in order to make herself feel useful on the farm was nothing to sneeze at either. And the telecommunication was still taking a toll on her mentally.

But seriously. It was getting ridiculous.

Justin and Trevor came through the back door just as Kara reached the kitchen. They were both smiling broadly at her and pulled her into their signature sandwiching embrace.

"What are you two so happy about?" Kara tried to wiggle out of their grasp. There was no way she could possibly have sex with them again without eating first. She knew that look. The hungry coy look they gave her when they wanted her body.

For the past eight weeks she felt like she'd done nothing

but have sex. She wasn't complaining. These men were her world, and they'd been right about the bond. She couldn't get enough of them. She was as insatiable as them. When would the fervor let up? They'd implied it would slow down. She wouldn't be as driven to have them twenty-four hours a day eventually, but when would that be? No one had quite answered the burning question.

"Don't look at me like that." Kara scrambled free and headed toward the smell of bacon and eggs.

"Like what, hon?" Justin followed her so closely she could feel him breathing down her neck.

"Like you want to eat me," she stated. "I'm so tired. And so hungry. What time is it anyway?"

"Almost noon." Trevor beat Kara to the stove and filled a plate for her.

"What?" Kara spun around to find the clock on the microwave. "How the hell could I possibly sleep so long?"

Silence.

When she swung back around, Trevor held out a plate of food, and Justin leaned against the counter with his arms folded across his chest. Both were grinning ear to ear.

"Yeah, we've been meaning to talk to you." Trevor ushered her over to the table and set the plate down before pulling out a chair and manhandling her gently into it.

"What? It's your fault. Both of you. You keep me up all hours pawing me and, and…" Kara paused while the two of them sat across from her, still smiling their shit-eating grins.

"Kara, you're pregnant." Justin spoke the foreign words.

She stared at him for a moment. "No. No. I can't be. I…" *What?* She'd been having sex day and night for two months without any protection. She'd never refilled her birth control pills after graduation. Justin and Trevor had told her oral contraception didn't work against shapeshifters anyway. Why didn't she think of it? Of course she was pregnant. *"Pregnant?* Oh my *God.* Seriously?"

Kara stared back and forth between both men, stunned.

"We couldn't be happier," Trevor said. "And wolf pregnancies tend to make you more tired than humans. You're going to do a lot of sleeping. It's okay. It's perfectly normal."

Kara couldn't catch her breath. "I'm going to have a baby?" As the news sunk in, she felt a smile form on her face.

"That's generally what happens about nine months after you get pregnant, yes." Justin laughed. "We love you so much, hon." Justin moved around the table and lifted Kara up to hug her.

From behind she had the warm hands of Trevor reaching around her waist to land on her now-flat belly. "Yes, we do, babe. We adore you. And you're going to be the mother of our children."

Kara could only choke back a sob of happiness and reach into their minds. *"I love you both so much it hurts."*

AUTHOR'S NOTE

I hope you've enjoyed this first book in the Wolf Masters series. Please enjoy the following excerpt from the second book in the series, *Lindsey's Wolves*.

LINDSEY'S WOLVES

WOLF MASTERS, BOOK TWO

"I met someone."

"Lindsey, that's great. Where? When?" Kara's voice held the excitement Lindsey had expected.

She switched the cell phone to her other ear and took a deep breath. "At the grocery store, yesterday actually."

Kara laughed. "The grocery store? How romantic." Her voice dripped sarcasm. "What's his name?"

"Alejandro." She tried not to make it sound too dreamy, but it was hard to utter the name without doing so. *My friends call me "Alex,"* he'd said, but with his sexy accent and looks, Lindsey couldn't think of him by that nickname yet.

"Alejandro? Is he Hispanic?"

"Spanish actually. His family owns a vineyard in Spain. Moved here a few months ago to join his cousins on the family farm."

"Farm?"

"Yeah. Strangest thing. That's part of why I called. Alejandro's aunt and uncle own a dairy farm not far from where you are. Isn't that a coincidence? I thought Trevor or Justin might know them."

"That *is* crazy."

"Yeah, what are the chances either of us city girls would meet a man who owns a dairy farm? Let alone both of us."

"What's his last name? I'll ask the guys if they know him."

"Ramos, but his cousins have a different name. It's his mother's side or something like that. Thompson."

"Hmm, doesn't ring a bell. But I don't know all the neighbors. I'll ask. So, you just met him yesterday?"

"Yes, it was a long day. Suffice it to say, my ice cream melted…in the cart." Lindsey laughed.

"Seriously? You just stood in the aisle talking to a guy?"

"Yeah, pretty much." Lindsey inhaled before continuing. "Listen, Kara, I was hoping you could tell me what it was like when you met Justin, and well Trevor too, I guess. Did you know he was the one right away?"

Kara paused too. Lindsey could hear her breathing over the line. "Lin? Is this serious?"

"I guess. I mean, it seems like it. He…sort of knocked me off my feet. And I believe it was mutual. Do you think it's possible? I mean to run into someone in a grocery store and then feel like…like you've known them forever?"

"It's possible. Yes."

"Did you?"

"Yes, but—"

Lindsey didn't give her a chance to finish. "It's just so weird. I haven't ever felt like this before. You know, giddy." She repressed another chuckle.

Kara didn't. She laughed. "Maybe he's the *one*. When are you seeing him again?"

"Seven. Dinner. Kara I want you to meet him. I don't know anyone else who could possibly think this wasn't just too weird. Including me. My hands are shaking just thinking about it."

"Because you really like him? Or because you're scared?"

"Both." Kara was one of the few people who knew a lot about Lindsey's past.

"Sounds about right. When I met Justin…well, you were there."

Now it was Lindsey's turn to laugh, hard. "Yeah, you'd known him for what? Eight minutes before Jess and I found you guys playing tongue hockey against the outside wall of Boot Scooters?" She couldn't keep the mirth from her voice. "You were dazed after that, and you still are. That's why I called. I need you to tell me what you felt. Tell me I'm not crazy."

"You definitely aren't crazy, Lin. And…I don't think I can quite describe how I felt. Warm. Happy. I couldn't stop smiling. Remember when you guys were helping me get ready for our date the next night, and you made me wear that slinky dress? I thought I'd die. It so wasn't me. But, man did I feel sexy in it. And it was worth the look on Justin's face. And Trevor's."

"Did you meet Trevor that night?"

"Yep. I didn't realize the implications at the time, but yeah. He was at the house."

"I guess I'll have Jess doll me up tonight like we did you. Wish you were here."

"Me too, Lin. Hey, why don't you bring him by later, after dinner?"

Lindsey shuffled back and forth. She couldn't keep her feet still she was so wired. "That would be awesome. You could confirm if I'm crazy or not."

"I can confirm that right now. You aren't crazy. I'm sure it'll be fine. But if it makes you feel better, I'll have the guys check him out. Ask a few questions. Surely, someone knows him, or at least the family he's living with."

"Thanks, Kara."

A familiar knock sounded at the door, sending a chill down Lindsey's spine. Three firm raps. "Shit."

"What's the matter?"

"The Bible Trio is here again." She peeked through the edge of the curtain on the front window to verify her suspicions.

"Jeez. They've been by there a lot lately, haven't they?"

"Yeah, guess they're really intent on saving my soul. They won't take *no* for an answer. I've stopped opening the door. It's the end of my summer break. In just a few weeks I have to start working and enter the real world. I don't need them constantly putting a damper on my good times."

"I'm sorry, Lin. Ignore them. They'll get the hint one of these days."

"Thanks, Kara. I know they've been a pain in your and Jess's butts over the years too. I appreciate your support."

"No worries. Think about your date tonight instead. And stop by whenever you want. We'll have drinks or something. I'll make a dessert."

"Perfect."

"And, Lin, don't worry if you can't make it. I'll understand. If it just seems too weird, or you're having too much fun, just don't show."

"'Kay. Wish me luck."

Lindsey stood in front of her full-length mirror and couldn't believe the vision in front of her. "Is that even me?" she asked Jessica.

"It's you, all right. A little more makeup than usual. A few curls in that long straight hair. A tight dress. And *voila*." Jess sat cross-legged on Lindsey's bed, leaning forward over her knees with her chin on one hand. "You look to die for."

Lindsey wasn't sure. "Is it too much? I didn't look anything like this when I met him. Maybe he likes his women a bit more…plain."

"Girl, you never look 'plain,' so that can't be true. Even without makeup, hair in a ponytail, wearing sweats, you look like a tall cover model." Jessica ran a hand through her own short locks. "Wish I had your long, thick hair."

"Are you kidding? I'd kill for your sophisticated style." Jess always looked put-together, even first thing in the morning. Her short, dark hair with blonde-tipped highlights always appeared salon perfect. Multiple dainty diamond and hoop earrings added to her glamour.

"Whatever." Jess raised her eyebrows.

"Well, thanks for the ego boost." She twisted and turned to see the back of the dress. "Is it too short?"

"No. Stop worrying. It'll be great."

"Yoga pants, by the way."

"Huh?"

"I wasn't wearing sweats yesterday. Yoga pants."

They both laughed, and then Jessica turned serious. "I almost forgot to tell you. Those people came by again yesterday. I had words with them."

"Shit. Yesterday too? They were here this morning again. I didn't open the door. What did you tell them?"

"I said you were out and that you weren't interested. And would they please stop calling and stopping by."

"Not that it'll do any good, but thanks."

"No problem."

The doorbell rang.

Lindsey turned around with a gasp. She shook all thoughts of her unwanted visitors from her head. Tonight was her night, and she wasn't about to let her past ruin one second of her future. "He's here already. Mr. Prompt. I'll never be able to keep up with that."

"Stop worrying. He isn't taking you out because of your timeliness. He likes you." Jess jumped up and headed for the front door. "How 'bout we let him in?" Her chuckle echoed as she sped down the hallway.

Lindsey took one more look in the mirror. Jess had, for the last hour, painstakingly helped her arrange her normally pin-straight hair until it now cascaded around her face in ringlets. She did look good, she had to admit.

Who cares? It's just a date. Why did it seem like so much more?

Her dress was skimpy, by her standards, and black. Too short, but heck, you only live once. Hopefully, he'd find her long legs sexy.

Having very few occasions to wear heels, Lindsey carefully turned and stepped from the room, doing her best to avoid the piles of rejected clothes lying all over the floor. Hopefully, Alejandro wouldn't want to see her private space. She'd die of embarrassment right now.

When she came around the corner, she sucked in a breath at the sight of Alejandro's firm, sexy ass encased in perfect-fitting, black pants. The muscles in his thighs and butt made her want to squeeze them with her hands...or her legs...

In less than a heartbeat, he turned to face her, a huge smile on his face, probably from something corny Jess had said to entertain him.

"Lindsey, you look gorgeous." He stepped toward her, which was convenient since her legs had stopped working. She was frozen in the hallway several feet from him.

His gaze traveled the length of her, not ogling, but admiring, as he advanced. Lindsey stared at his handsome face. His soft brown hair was filled with blond highlights from the sun and it hung slightly too long, the thick waves swaying across his eyes. Perhaps he needed a trim, but she loved it that way. It was incredibly sexy the way he tossed it from his eyes as he leaned into her.

Startled by his unexpected proximity, Lindsey continued to hold her breath.

Alejandro casually reached for her elbows with his warm hands and leaned across first her left and then her right cheek, breathing a kiss over each.

Ah, you idiot. He's Spanish. It's a greeting, you dolt.

Chills coursed down Lindsey's skin from her neck clear to her feet. She gritted her teeth to avoid outright shivering at his touch, his scent. He smelled like summer, a hint of tropical sunscreen under the soap he'd showered with. And his hair, all those glorious locks, caressed her cheek as he pulled away. Whatever shampoo he'd used was perfect for him, a very masculine almost outdoorsy scent.

Lindsey cleared her throat, hoping her voice wouldn't squeak whenever she was finally able to say something coherent. "You too."

You too? Is that the best you can come up with? A degree in education with an emphasis in English and the best you could utter was, "you too?"

"*Gracias, mi alma.*"

Whatever *mi alma* meant, she loved the way it sounded rolling off his tongue. He'd have her any way he wanted if he kept using that sexy Spanish voice.

What was she thinking? She needed to slow down a bit. No way was she ready for an intense relationship. Her body was getting ahead of her mind just by his proximity. Sure, her shrink would tell her to go for it. Let loose. Move on with her life. But could she really do it? Could she slough off the first eighteen years of her life after four years of counseling?

"Are you ready?" His eyebrows rose in question, his palms still wrapped around her elbows, seeming to cover half her arms in their gentle warmth.

Lindsey had always been quite tan, but when she glanced down at their skin next to each other, she realized how much darker Alejandro was. Probably from working outside all summer. The sleeves of his deep purple dress shirt were meticulously folded up far enough to reveal his bronzed muscular forearms covered in a dusting of blond hair.

She couldn't help wondering if that same hair covered his chest or if he was smooth under his shirt. As she returned her gaze to his face, she paused at his neck. The top two buttons were undone, but not far enough to answer her question.

"Yes." It was going to be a short night if she didn't come up with anything more conversational.

He didn't seem to mind, however. His smile grew slowly across his face as if he were completely aware of her plight and found it amusing.

He couldn't be of course.

"Shall we?" Letting go of one elbow, he guided her toward the front door with the other.

Jessica was nowhere in sight. Not surprising. She never liked to interfere.

"Where are we going?" *Ah, a full sentence. And even apropos.*

"I thought we'd try that new Spanish restaurant across town. Do you know it?"

"No." *Does that count as a sentence also?* "But, it sounds wonderful."

"I hope it's authentic and not a disappointment. You never know about these places. I've heard good things about it, but not from anyone Spanish. We'd be taking our chances. Are you up for the adventure?"

"Absolutely. Even if it's not completely what you're used to, it will surely be delicious."

"We Spaniards are culinary snobs." He probably wasn't kidding, but his words were so gentle and his face so calm, she didn't believe he was capable of disappointment right now. A fact that made her feel pretty good.

Alejandro led her toward a brand new black Toyota truck parked in the street in front of the townhome she shared with Jessica. Ever since Kara moved out earlier in the summer, they hadn't bothered to get another roommate. They had both gotten teaching jobs locally and as soon as school started in a few weeks they'd be making enough money to handle the expenses. In the meantime, they were enjoying the last few weeks of summer, their last few leisurely weeks for what could be a long time.

Ever the gentleman, Alejandro opened the passenger door and held on to Lindsey's arm until she was situated inside. She felt like a princess in his care. Doted on. Appreciated.

American men never seemed quite so polite, or maybe that had been just her experience.

In any case, who cared? The man currently circling the hood of the truck was so suave she wanted to lean into him and soak up his tender warmth.

And his accent was so musical—like melted caramel it oozed over her every time he spoke. Especially when he spoke in Spanish. She'd taken four years of high school Spanish, but that barely got her by.

Maybe if she hung around Alejandro for a while, she'd actually learn something.

I hope so.

When he slid into the seat beside her, he started the

engine and then reached for her hand. "You truly are *bellísima* this evening, *querida*."

She got the idea. "Thank you." Lindsey was so comfortable with him. It seemed as though she'd known him a long time.

Of course, they'd spoken for about two hours last night. She felt like she truly did know him in some ways. Once they finally made it out of the grocery store, he helped her load her trunk, and they wandered into the coffee shop conveniently located next door to the supermarket. The lattes didn't come close to reaching Alejandro's coffee standards, but they still laughed and talked for so long, she'd lost track of time.

Alejandro's large hand enveloped Lindsey's small one now as they headed for the restaurant. She couldn't concentrate with his thumb rubbing circles across her palm. He was going to drive her mad. If there hadn't been a seat belt law, she'd have slid right up next to him and laid her head on his shoulder with no concern whatsoever for how forward that would be.

Truth be told, she couldn't wait to feel his soft lips caress her skin again. Last night, when he walked her to her practical Honda Accord, he'd pressed her back into the driver's door, wrapped her face in his palms, and kissed her to oblivion. Sure, it had started out slow and hesitant, the faint hint of coffee mingling with her own, but then he angled his head to one side, pressed his body against hers, and licked the seam between her lips until she opened for him on a moan.

The episode was so erotic, a book could have been written about that kiss alone. Her entire body trembling with need, she'd gripped his forearms until her nails nearly dug into the skin. After what seemed like an eternity, he gradually pulled away, raining kisses along her cheeks before settling his forehead against hers.

"*Mañana entonces, querida*? Until tomorrow?"

Why did his words in Spanish sound so much more lyrical? Those beautiful words meant "until tomorrow?"

"Yes." It was all she'd been able to articulate at the time, and she hadn't improved much since then.

If only he would kiss her like that again…

And please, God, let me enjoy this without enduring flashbacks from my childhood.

She deserved it. It was time to move on.

Hot SEAL, Red Wine

Hot SEAL, Australian Nights

Hot SEAL, Cold Feet

Dark Falls:

Dark Nightmares

Club Zodiac:

Training Sasha

Obeying Rowen

Collaring Brooke

Mastering Rayne

Trusting Aaron

Claiming London

Sharing Charlotte

Taming Rex

Tempting Elizabeth

Club Zodiac Box Set One

Club Zodiac Box Set Two

The Art of Kink:

Pose

Paint

Sculpt

Arcadian Bears:

Grizzly Mountain

Grizzly Beginning

Grizzly Secret

Grizzly Promise

Grizzly Survival

Grizzly Perfection

Arcadian Bears Box Set One

Arcadian Bears Box Set Two

Sleeper SEALs:

Saving Zola

Spring Training:

Catching Zia

Catching Lily

Catching Ava

Spring Training Box Set

The Underground series:

Force

Clinch

Guard

Submit

Thrust

Torque

The Underground Box Set One

The Underground Box Set Two

Saving Sofia (Special Forces: Operations Alpha)

Wolf Masters series:

Kara's Wolves

Lindsey's Wolves

Jessica's Wolves

Alyssa's Wolves

Tessa's Wolf

Rebecca's Wolves

Melinda's Wolves

Laurie's Wolves

Amanda's Wolves

Sharon's Wolves

Wolf Masters Box Set One

Wolf Masters Box Set Two

Claiming Her series:

The Rules

The Game

The Prize

Emergence series:

Bound to be Taken

Bound to be Tamed

Bound to be Tested

Bound to be Tempted

Emergence Box Set

The Fight Club series:

Come

Perv

Need

Hers

Want

Lust

The Fight Club Box Set One

The Fight Club Box Set Two

Wolf Gatherings series:

Tarnished

Dominated

Completed

Redeemed

Abandoned

Betrayed

Wolf Gatherings Box Set One

Wolf Gathering Box Set Two

Durham Wolves series:

Rescue in the Smokies

Fire in the Smokies

Freedom in the Smokies

Stand Alone Books:

Blind with Love

Guarding the Truth

Out of the Smoke

Abducting His Mate

Three's a Cruise

Wolf Trinity

Frostbitten

A Princess for Cale/A Princess for Cain

ABOUT THE AUTHOR

Becca Jameson is a USA Today best-selling author of over 90 books. She is most well-known for her Wolf Masters series and her Fight Club series. She currently lives in Houston, Texas, with her husband and her Goldendoodle. Two grown kids pop in every once in a while too! She is loving this journey and has dabbled in a variety of genres, including paranormal, sports romance, military, and BDSM.

A total night owl, Becca writes late at night, sequestering herself in her office with a glass of red wine and a bar of dark chocolate, her fingers flying across the keyboard as her characters weave their own stories.

During the day--which never starts before ten in the morning!--she can be found jogging, running errands, or reading in her favorite hammock chair!

…where Alphas dominate…

Becca's Newsletter Sign-up:
http://beccajameson.com/newsletter-sign-up

Join my Facebook fan group, Becca's Bibliomaniacs, for the most up-to-date information, random excerpts while I work, giveaways, and fun release parties!

Facebook Fan Group:
https://www.facebook.com/groups/BeccasBibliomaniacs/

Contact Becca:
www.beccajameson.com
beccajameson4@aol.com

facebook.com/becca.jameson.18

twitter.com/beccajameson

instagram.com/becca.jameson

bookbub.com/authors/becca-jameson

goodreads.com/beccajameson

amazon.com/author/beccajameson

Printed in Great Britain
by Amazon

64694115R00142